STOCK AND FLOW

STOCK AND FLOW

Short Fiction

Matt Raskie

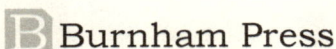Burnham Press

Burnham Press – Atlanta, Georgia

Printed in the United States of America

Library of Congress Control Number: 2015904934

ISBN-10: 0-692-41624-2
ISBN-13: 978-0-692-41624-2

BurnhamPress.com

To Susan and Martin

CONTENTS

TRACKSIDE

I bet on Chilly Pepper because she said not to. Said the jockey Marconi's been runnin' his horses like donkeys these last few races. Said he'd run it flat. The owners knew it. The riders knew it. Hell, even she knew it. But I bet on him anyway.

She was rich, this one. As if that mattered somehow. But that was the way it started—because she was rich. But money doesn't make you right, no matter how hard you think it. Anyway, what would I know? I've got none of my own.

These people think they know horses. Maybe they do. Or maybe they just make it up as they go along like we all do with everythin' else. No, I remember she said somethin' about growin' up ridin' 'em. Maybe she does know somethin'. The odds, of course, show him as favorite. Chilly Pepper. I always bet with the odds. Always have. Tells you somebody knows somethin'. Well, maybe that doesn't mean nothin', but I put what I have left on him to win. I'll do what I want with my money, I tell myself. But it's not my money. She just let me play with some of hers. In the end, of course, he comes in fourth. Runs it flat just like she said. I watch him in close that last quarter mile. Started out front. Then that last quarter mile, jockey runs him so flat it doesn't even fool me. And I don't know 'bout horses.

My ticket falls in little bits to the ground. My heel follows and digs it into the wet grass. It's better off there, anyway.

"Who'd you bet on?" she asks.

"Seven to win," I say. Seven came in third. Couldn't even admit it, I'm that damn *do-mesticated*.

Tickets on the ground scatter like leaves in fall. It is fall, I guess, but the leaves haven't gone yet. Just white tickets everywhere. Everywhere you step.

Up in the stands the crowd is up before the next race. We've got twenty minutes, but I'm outta cash. Just enough for a sip of somethin'. Just enough to keep me respectable in this crowd.

"Did you see how Hay Bonnet inched up at the end to win?" she asks.

She isn't talkin' to me. She's talkin' to Annie. Annie's the one that really knows 'bout horses. Has a few racin'

today. Or, Daddy does, anyway. He's way up in a box somewhere. Never met the guy. Never mean to.

All these people down here own 'em, too. Not me
though. My pop used to say no one could ever really own a
horse. Believed in John Wayne and all that. Used to tell me
all about horses when mom was workin' Saturdays mop-
pin' up at the hospital and he'd have nothin' else to do but
take me with him to the track. Out from Brooklyn on the
train. I was just a kid then. Used to bet our rent money. But
he did all right. Knew the trainers pretty well, I guess. It's
the trainers that know the horses best. Or know how the
jockeys'll run 'em.

"You should have bet on Hay Bonnet like she did,
Emmett," Annie says to me. I turn and give her a look without tryin' to, and then I try to take it back, but it's already
out there. I kinda like Annie. Wish I'd gotten her instead.
Annie's not so good lookin', but she's got some kind of
mouth on her. I like her for it. Get a couple drinks in her
and she'll have you crackin' all night. Gets prettier with a
couple drinks, too. She's all right.

"He's just mad 'cause he lost," says Sam. Sam's the one
I'm with. The one with the money. Bigger pile anyway.
Never liked her name so she chopped it in half. Makes
her sound like a boy, but she's nothin' like it. Prissy as they
get. Plat'num blonde hair, pink dresses, pink shoes, all of
it. All of it pink. Even got pink bows in her hair. I don't say
nothin' and just force a smile. Can't be bothered. Where
the hell's that waiter for the damn drinks anyway?

This crowd isn't what I'm used to. Met Sam in summer at a bar and she took to me 'cause I'm tall. Told me right there she liked me 'cause I'm blond and I'm tall. Guess that's enough for some girls. My pop always said that'd get me somewhere, bein' tall. He was pretty short himself. Don't know where I got it from. Guess bein' tall got me here, anyways. Sam's a tall girl, too, I guess. For a girl. I got almost a foot on her. Bony, too. Never liked 'em tall and bony, but I'm not picky. Usually like 'em just right with a little meat on 'em. I've had worse. And this one's got money, so I'll stick it out for a while and see what I can get. Then it's back to my crowd when she's done with me. No use kiddin' myself with any of that.

"I'm going to go get my winnings," she says. "Want to come?"

She won all of ten dollars. Only bet two. You'd think these people with all their money would throw more down. I know I would. Throw it all down! Take the big cardboard check home. But they don't. Maybe that's why they've got it and I don't.

"Nah, I'll just stay here. I'm done bettin' for t'day."

Before I can finish, they're gone. Annie and Sam. Gone to get their whole damn ten dollars.

"Get us some drinks, will you?" Sam calls back.

They're gone in a second and I flag down a waiter and order my whisky and splash of soda. And another splash of whisky. And two drinks for the girls. What were they drinkin'? Vodka somethin'. Vodka sodas I think. Lime. No lime. I forget. Get 'em somethin' with vodka.

"This is for mine," I say. I hand him what cash I've got left. Not much. "They'll be back to get the rest."

He's gone in a second, too, and then it's just me alone with all these prissy ladies with their big hats and their uptight gents, and to keep them from tryin' to talk to me 'cause I can't stand minglin' with 'em I find a seat in a wooden chair and lean back in it and grab a half empty plastic glass of cheap champagne sittin' next to me, wishin' I had some shade to cool off in.

"Excuse me!" says a big fat woman in a big fat hat standin' above me, blockin' out the sun. "Those are our seats."

"Sorry, ma'am," I say with the snootiest Mr. Belvedere I can muster. There's lots of seats around. It's just her alone though, and I think she meant it for both halves of her, one for each cheek.

I get back up and go back to the rail I was leanin' on. It was good to sit down, if only for a sec. Only so much my legs can take in the sun. And my back's already feelin' it. Always did when I stood up too long. Never lasted long on school field trips. This one loves museums, Sam does. Studied "The History of Art" or some damn thing. Didn't know you could study that. Just old pictures, I guess. So my back takes it every time.

The crew's just comin' 'round the finish with the tractor and rakes the dirt down smooth. Last race was right up close, but the next one'll be out on the turf, just off a bit from where we are now. I watch the tractor pull out the startin' gate across the field, and the horses are out in front of us with their handlers, and the jockeys bein' weighed. Everyone with their colors on. Pink and brown and yellow and black and blue. The grass is all combed down in rows out in the middle there. This racetrack's gotta be a hundred years old. Belmont. 1905 I think the sign said. Yeah, more'n a hundred years old. My pop used to come here before he died, and I think he used to come here with his own pop before that. Dodgers games were too expensive with the hot dogs and beer and all, and there was no money in it, so they used to take the money they had and try to double or triple it here. Coulda bet in the city, of course, but I think he liked comin' out here himself. That's how my pop got in good with the trainers. Grew up with 'em when their own pops were the trainers. Then he'd give back a little. Worked out well for everybody. My pop never had much to bet with, but he did all right. Never missed rent. Mom never knew about it, anyway.

I never came on my own, though, after he died. This is the first time I've been out here since he passed. That was thirteen years ago. Feels good to be back. Didn't even know how much I'd missed it 'til I came back and smelled the track and the wet grass. Feels good.

The girls are back with their winnings. All singles. Got paid out in singles. And the waiter's back with the drinks.

"You didn't pay?" she asks. She knows I didn't, but she asks anyway. Real loud so Annie hears. So everybody hears. Even the fat lady with the big fat hat takin' up two seats. Everybody hears.

"Nope," I say. "Didn't have enough cash on me." She knows I'm skint and even worse I'm cheap, but she feels like holdin' it out there every chance she gets. I don't try to hide it, so I say it real loud, too. She pulls out her pocketbook and folds out as many bills as she has. Flips through them twice. Twice, just to make the point. Twenties and fifties and hundreds and everythin' she's got. Makes it real known to me and to the waiter she's never worked a day in her life. Never will. Not like me. Not like the waiter. I knew she'd pull that. Does it every chance she gets with me.

So I'm in a pretty foul mood when the next race starts, but I feel good with the whisky I took down and the other one I ordered on Sam's tab. No money on the race, but I know the girls've got some, and I know they'll do all right. Annie knows her horses.

"Come on Money Plays!" she yells. They both yell it and they both have money on the tan filly. "Come on Money!" It's one of the horses Annie knows and she put five dollars on her. Whole five dollars.

Well, Money Plays wins and they're all excited. Just three-to-one odds. Nothin' to get real excited about.

"You should just bet with Sam," Annie says to me. I had my back turned to the race and only caught the last hundred yards. Wanted to give my back a rest against the rail.

"Well, maybe next time," I say with the help of Mr. Belvedere, "when she lets me have my allowance." Not that I mean anythin' by it, but it comes out that way.

Well Sam looks at me for a good long time while the crowd cheers the win. White tickets fall to the ground like all mine have, and Sam just looks at me the way she does. But this time it's different. Different in a way that tells me somethin', and I know what's comin'. I can see it in her eyes. I've seen it before from her, but not like this. Not this bad. This time it's different.

She looks away. Her eyes look to the ground and I see through her sunglasses she's about to cry. But she doesn't cry. Her lips barely open. "Just go," she says under her breath and turns away.

I look at her for a second just to see if she means it, still leanin' against the rail.

"Damn it, Emmett. Just go!" she says again without lookin' at me.

Well there's not much I can do but push myself off the rail and start walkin' toward the gate. I don't even look back to see if she does means it. I know she does. I hear Annie say somethin' as if she can do somethin' about it. Annie's known us together for a while now. Few weeks anyway. I know Annie likes me around. I wish I'd gotten her. Wouldn't have such problems.

"Come on, Sam..." she says. "He didn't..."

But I did mean it, and I don't hear anythin' after that. Just keep walkin'.

At the gate they ask if I want my hand stamped.

"No," I say. "I think that's it for me." At least I got myself a few drinks today.

As I pass out the gate the crowd fades to a whisper, as if they'd just disappeared or a big door had closed. Just beyond the gate there's a taxi file. The drivers are all out sittin' on the grass talkin' to their buds.

"Where you goin'?" the first one asks.

"Eh, I got no money."

The man turns back to finish his story without skippin' a breath. I walk over to where the trains come in special for the races. Used to come here by train when I was a kid. Next one's forty minutes out, so I sit there on the worn wood bench and rest my legs and stretch my back and thumb through the race program I'd had in my jacket pocket. Never liked wearin' a jacket. I think about tossin' it, but she did spend a buck on it. Liked to dress me up. Like I was a damn Ken doll. Maybe I can use it again. Best clothes I got.

No one else around. They're about to start the seventh. I can hear the announcer. I follow down the names as he calls 'em out. Woulda put my money on Teemo if I had any. Three-year-old colt. Best odds. I always bet with the odds. Wonder if Annie woulda picked Teemo.

It's a long ride back into the city. Train makes every stop on weekends. Conductor comes by, but I keep movin' back to the next car and then the next and then duck into the bathroom as the train pulls into Penn. Don't have any money for a ticket. Learned that from my pop. Conductor gives me a nod as I step off—I do the same. The games we play.

No place left to go but P.J.'s on Third. Midtown. Long walk from Penn. But I know Chip'll be there. I know he will. Yesterday was payday. Chip stacks boxes at a grocery store, and if I know Chip he'll be at P.J.'s today. Just hope he hasn't spent it all yet. Usually just gets him through the weekend. Maybe I can get a drink. Chip owes me a few.

Back to my own crowd, I guess.

HOTEL BONITA

He pulled up to the counter and waited for the man to notice him from the back. There was no bell. A tramp stood silently with her arms folded a few feet away smoking the butt of a cigarette, watching him tensely. She had an old, faded-to-green dragon tattoo down a leg strapped in shiny black leather heels. Her stiff, curly hair reminded him of cigarette girls in casinos—strippers and showgirls too old to make it any other way. When the man came up to the counter and asked him his name he said it was Davis and that he wanted to pay in cash.

"Good," the man behind the desk said, "because the card machine's broken and we don't take checks."

The man gave him his key and continued his conversation with the woman standing there as if there had been no break. "He's just a crank..." the man went on. "Old cranky bastard."

"Is the area safe?" Davis interrupted the man behind the counter.

"Sure," he said. "Only thing you need to watch out for is the cops."

"Why's that?" Davis asked.

"They'll getcha for nothin'. County just cut the budget and they went short on citations last quarter. Runnin' outta money. It was in the paper. Be careful crossin' the street. They'll give you a ticket even if it's just flashin' Don't Walk. No way to argue—you'll end up payin' anyway."

Up in his room, which he reached clumsily by stairs with his two large suitcases, he found a Murphy bed, a table, and a folded metal chair. There was a separate room that turned out to be a bathroom with a sink, a toilet, and a shower. He was glad to have his own shower. There was a common bathroom for the hall next door to his room, but the other rooms were full, so the man at the counter gave him the same rate. A sign on the back of the door said the pool was closed. He didn't worry about that. The last thing he wanted to do in a place like this was use the pool.

There was a brick wall in the room on one side. Looking closer, he found it was fake decorative brick that rubbed off when you touched it. Why'd they even go to the trouble? Must've been an all right place way back. He opened the window and leaned his head out and looked across the street. It was dark, but across the street was a row of bars with music and people shouting. It was a warm night. People would be out. He looked down the street and found a mortuary to the right. Another room faced his on the left, and as he looked that way the window shade went down abruptly. He pulled his head back in and shut the window only halfway so the air could still come in.

The Murphy bed was behind a curtain along the wall. He pulled the curtain back and pulled the bed down that was strapped in tight, and there was just enough room in the place to pull it down and ease yourself around it. He had to move his luggage out of the way to get it down all the way. He lay on the bed on top of the sheets, and it was a full foot shorter than he was. The room smelled like moldy cedar and reminded him of a cigar box. There was the faint but unmistakable sweet odor of pipe smoke rising from a room below. He would have gotten up to shut the window, but he had no energy left from the trip. And besides, it was too hot anyway.

He left the room and found the hooker still in the lobby alone with her arms folded. She was out of cigarettes. He thought about nodding hello to her and then thought better of it. He didn't need the trouble. Around the corner from the hotel he found a thrift store and a pawn shop, and around the corner from these there was a Chinese restaurant and a tropical fish store. All closed for the night. He had no need for them anyway. The streets were narrow and the blocks so short that in a few minutes he had circled back on himself and found the hotel again. It was a quiet town. Dull. Far from the big city he knew. He wouldn't like it here. As time went on it would wear on him, and he knew it. When he saw the hotel he remembered he had seen a sign for a liquor store somewhere down a side street and went back and bought the cheapest bottle of wine. Not much more than a buck.

The train tracks ran just down the street from the hotel, and as he climbed the stairs back up to his room he heard the train horn blow loud as it raced and thundered by. He wondered where the train was going, and a few days later he would see that it was going either to or from San Antonio. The factory was just on the other side of the tracks. He would walk by tomorrow and check it out. It was a Saturday night. He started work on Monday—a job that Benny back in Chicago had been able to swing for him. At least it was something.

The night was hot, and he had no money to go out and get drunk in the bars where it would be cool with the air conditioning. He went back up to his room and took off his shirt and slacks and sat in the metal folding chair with his feet on the bed to read from a book he had found in the bus station. He liked how books packaged things so neatly. There was a beginning and an end. No mess or anything after you were done. When you were done, you were done, and that was it. No more.

He pulled up the bottle from the paper bag and found he had no way to open it. He had no corkscrew or knife and thought about going down to ask the man behind the counter for something—but he thought better of it because the hooker was down there and he knew she would get the wrong idea seeing him again. He thought about breaking the neck of the bottle, but there were no cups to pour the wine into, and he didn't want the noise and the bits of glass. He found a hard plastic pen in his suitcase and pounded the cork down into the bottle with a splash of red wine back out over his hands. He took a big swig of the warm liquid and felt better. It tasted like spoiled fruit, but it was better than nothing; and when half the bottle was gone he didn't mind the taste anymore.

He fell asleep that night on the hot bed with the sticky air around him. He didn't want to be there. Life hadn't exactly made the turns he'd expected these last few years. But there was no way around it and nowhere else to go. On the nightstand lay seventeen crumpled dollars that had been laid out flat—not enough for the girl downstairs, he'd decided, if he wanted the room for another night and a few bites before the job started. And maybe another bottle of wine. Tomorrow he would start looking for a cheaper place to stay.

MARCELA

The sun had broken the horizon but had not yet risen above the hills on the other side of the bight. Stark rays of light spread out in a fan in the early humid haze and struck gray decaying clouds from the night's storm that were creeping off slowly toward the west. The blues of the shallow sea in the lagoon he had known from the day before were dull and muddled in the morning light. He wiped the dew that had settled on his skin as he leaned forward and knew without feeling that she was no longer lying there next to him.

It was no more than a hundred yards to the water over coarse sand that was now scattered with fronds and dead mangrove leaves from the night's storm, and as he dove into the cool water he washed away the sleep and the night and the cruel words that had come from her drunken lips. The cruel words that came every night. There would be no apology, no mention of what was said. He rubbed the water over his face and through his long sun-bleached hair. He opened his eyes in the salty water and felt the pleasant sting. Anchored far off in the distance was the boat, which they had not visited for three or four days. This afternoon, he thought, he might paddle out to reset the anchor chain, to see if the wind had loosened any of the hatches, and to gather a few cans of food for the beach. But from where he stood everything looked fine, and he might not get back out there for another day or so. Nothing seemed urgent now. Nothing required his attention.

As he returned and approached the hut, he saw Marcela sitting there in a white plastic chair smoking a cigarette. She looked past him into the distance, not seeing him. He said nothing to her as he passed.

Inside, he pulled down the smaller of his two spearguns from the wall and inspected it from butt to tip. The trigger was rusted but would pull fine in the water. He would just need to keep it well pointed a moment longer without raising the tip as he pulled. The stock was worn and scarred, but solid. Two of the surgical tube bands had broken, leaving only one that was growing stale from the salt and the sun. It still had a few shots left in it. The spear shaft was straight and smooth, but the tip was rusted and needed to be filed. His sharpening stone was still on the

17

boat. The single spring-loaded barb was rusted over, and he knew it would do little to keep a strong fish on if he hit it off the spine. He glanced up at the better six-footer, but he decided it was too cumbersome for the two or three small snapper he was after for lunch. From the three-legged table he grabbed his oval purge mask and his dive knife and belt and was back out the door toward the water.

Marcela saw him walk by but did not look up. She was still holding her same cigarette, though it had burned down and she had not yet brought it to her lips. Though there was no reason to, she would wait until he was gone before she would get another drink.

He hit the water with a soft splash and had made it thirty yards or so before he came up for air. Once he did, he stood on the sand up to his chest and readjusted his mask and felt to make sure his knife was still there in its sheath. This part of the lagoon was shallow and sandy. The few dozen fish that had scattered before him when he first dove in were wary and skittish out over the open sand with no place for cover, keeping their distance just beyond his reach. He wasn't after these fish anyway. A hundred yards out into the deeper water ran a coral ledge that would afford him the cover he needed. The larger fish were there as well, if he wanted to take one.

The sun was now on his back, and as he kicked out toward the reef he was growing warm with his movement. His mouth was dry from the rum the night before, and he wished now that he had tied a bottle of fresh water to his belt. But he was strong from his many months in the water, and when he floated above the reef a few minutes later he was not out of breath and it seemed that his thirst had left him. Yet, he leaned back and floated there for a minute to calm his heart. It was not a deep dive—only twenty feet to the top of the coral heads, and thirty feet to the sandy bottom—but he wanted his blood slowed so that he could stay down as long as possible.

His first dive was meant only to assess the area. He breathed slowly and took three long, deep breaths and then broke the surface into the silent world below. As he kicked downward he bent with the butt of the speargun in his stomach and strung the rubber cord back and placed the wire apex into the notched shaft of the spear. Then he continued downward along the reef to the ledges that had now grown familiar. He had come out here once or twice each day since they had first arrived. And each day he had discovered a new ledge, a new cave, or a new overhang where larger and fatter grouper lay hiding. But he was not after these large fish today. He only wanted enough for them to eat, and he liked the challenge of the smaller fish. The smaller snapper swam in schools, and he liked swimming through the schools as they parted and re-merged around him. Marcela was not eating now. She had not eaten in several days. He cooked for her each day, but she seemed only to survive on cigarettes and straight rum. He said nothing to her about this. She would eat if she wanted to, he thought. But each day he threw her plate out for the gulls when it remained there for hours untouched, collecting flies. Down below, he found the spot near a familiar overhang from where he would take his shots. Then he rose to the surface to regain his breath.

Even the quiet sounds of the wind and the waves at the surface made him crave the world below him. He wanted nothing more than to remain down there forever. If only his lungs did not require air. If only he could breathe the water as the fish did. These were the thoughts that consumed his days as he swam and walked along the beach—his desire for another world, which he could only visit, but which would only destroy him if he tried to remain too long.

On his second dive, he kicked his way straight past the coral heads down to the sandy bottom below. There, he dug his free hand deep into the sand and grabbed the sand and coarse gravel and shells and waved them into the water above him as his fingers slowly parted. Instantly, the small schools of snapper and grunts that had scattered away from him as he dove returned and darted into the cloud of sand, searching for food. He moved to position himself a few feet away on the sea floor and sat on his knees with the shaft of the spear aimed into the center of the cloud. He eyed a foot-long yellowtail, and as he watched it turn its side to him he pulled the trigger and felt the shock of the band propelling the shaft through the water and the recoil against his hands. The school of fish jolted away, but he knew from the sound through the water that he had hit his fish. He knew he needed air, and he kicked up to the surface with the gun trailing at his side.

As he rose, he felt the burn in his lungs and the swell of the air inside of him. He released his breath slowly and saw the bubbles rise before him, surrounding his body and tickling his darkened skin. When he broke the surface, he inhaled deeply and gasped several times for fresh air. His chest heaved in and out as he felt his blood renewed.

There at the surface, he floated calmly for a minute as his hands instinctively pulled the line from the gun to the spear shaft. He felt the snapper kicking at the end, impaled by the spear, and he liked the feel of the fish's futile fight. Yet, if the barb had not deployed, he may lose this fish; but there was no lack of fish to shoot below. He pulled the line up to him and found that the shaft had gone clear through the fish and the fish was several inches up the thin line. He floated on his back and worked the line and spear out of the fish, then he clipped the fish to the short monofilament stringer on his belt and reloaded the gun.

Another dive and he hit the sea floor and threw up the sand again. This time, many larger fish, which had been attracted by the fuss, surrounded the last of the thin cloud of sand that still hovered there. As soon as he threw the sand he swam a few feet closer to a ledge and watched as the larger fish moved in. He had a clear shot at a ten-pound grouper, but he was not out here for her. Not today. He waited for another foot-long snapper and shot. But this time the shaft caught the fish near the tail and bounced upward, leaving a nick in the fish as the whole group scattered. Cursing but laughing, he returned slowly to the surface.

The temptation was there, when he reached the surface, to use the snapper at his belt as bait. He could take it down, slash it with his dive knife on the bottom, leave it, and return to the surface. Then, when he would dive again, the larger fish would be coming in for it as the smaller schools fought over the floating scraps. But he reminded himself that he only needed one more decent snapper for lunch. There was no need for a bigger fish. Still, the temptation remained, as it always did.

He dove again and immediately took cover without going in to throw the sand. The schools were already swarming, and there were several larger fish easily within reach. There was no need to go in and run the risk of scattering them. Instead, he knelt on a coral head, aimed, and shot an identical foot-long yellowtail. He could take his time and retrieve it to his belt down below since the air in his lungs was still fresh. He quickly reeled the line in hand-over-hand, and a moment later he had two fish at his side. He placed the shaft into the speargun and locked it in place, but he did not reload the cord. Instead, he sat there for a moment and watched the cloud of fish before him. Some had scattered on his shot, but they had quickly returned to look for food that was not there. In the corner of his eye, he caught several larger figures moving in the distance. He knew what they were. He knew it was the blacktips, but there was no fear in him. These curious sharks had only come to investigate. They sensed the energy of the swarm of fish pulsing through the water, and they tasted the blood of the two snapper. As he started to feel the air burn in his lungs, he pushed off the coral head and floated unhurriedly toward the surface. He watched below, and as he moved off, the blacktips moved in below him as he rose above them. He knew they would not follow him up, even with the two freshly-killed snapper at his side.

When he reached the shore, he stepped onto the sand and felt the weight of the upper world return to him as he tramped through the small waves. He felt heavy and awkward on land, and again his mind went to the life he had left below the surface. He wanted to return. He wanted to go back down and remain there. It was the world he truly wanted. The sun on his back was hot, and he wanted now only the cool of the water below.

He approached the shack and saw that Marcela had not moved from where he had left her. But when he saw the empty glass in her hand he knew that she had indeed been up. There was a newly-lit cigarette between her fingers, and this time she looked up at him when he passed, but she did not say a word. Nor did he. As he entered the door he thought he saw the faintest hint of an approving smile on her face when she saw the fish. Maybe she would eat today, he thought. Maybe today she would break. He took the fish from his belt and tossed them into an empty foam cooler on the floor. He rubbed the specks of wet sand that still clung to his forearms. Then he reached up and poured himself some rum into a dirty glass and took a long, slow sip. He let it burn his tongue and breathed its warmth out through his nose. Then he turned and stared blankly for several minutes through the door toward the bright shore and toward the sounds of the waves and the wind in the palms. Maybe today will be a good day, he said to himself. He nodded several times and felt the burn of the rum in his mouth and the warmth of the air on his wet skin. Yes, he said, maybe today will be a good day.

SUNDOWN

"God damn it! We're lost, Im!" grumbled Chad under his breath, loud enough for them all to hear. "God damn it!" He closed his eyes and sighed deeply two or three times for effect. "God damn it, Im!"

He spun around on his heels and walked a few steps to the east along the dry dirt road, stood for a long minute looking into the distance, then turned on his heels again and walked a few steps back and stopped. He repeated this in several directions, each time muttering "God damn it" softer and softer under his breath until they could no longer hear him.

Imogen and Sebastian stood there silently. They knew they had to let Chad do this. They knew to just let him be. It was the only way.

Chad wanted to be mad. They knew he wanted to be mad, and they knew he wanted them to know he was mad. But they were not really lost at all. Half a mile in the distance, across the hundreds of rows of green vines, they could all clearly see the main house of the winery lit up in the growing darkness. They were the only lights for miles in every direction. They knew exactly where they were.

But the sun was going down, and that meant it was time for Chad to be angry. Imogen and Sebastian knew this. It was nothing new. Chad was always fine all day, until sunset. Then he would find some reason to get angry—or no reason at all. But it was Chad's time to be mad, and they knew that, and they let it be.

And then Imogen would convince Chad to eat something, and then to have a drink. And then they would all have a drink, and then they would all drink too much—always too much. But they would all be happy for a while, and that's when things were good. And Sebastian always wanted things to remain as they were at that precise moment, before all the rest came. And he knew Imogen wanted that, too.

And then, when they had all had too much, that's when Chad would get really angry. There would be yelling. Doors would slam. More yelling and more slamming. And when the last door had slammed and when the muffled yelling had stopped and there was only silence, that's when Sebastian wanted to tear down the walls and destroy Chad and liberate Imogen, because the silence meant only one thing—that the girl he desired more than anything in the world was being had by another. And he despised Chad for that, and Imogen would never leave Chad, and Chad would never let her go.

They had taken the earliest bus that morning from downtown Buenos Aires to Bahía Blanca that had left at ten past four in the morning. They were drunk because they had stayed up all night for the bus so they would not miss it. It was a full seven-hour ride, and the bus was empty except for the few household servants and dishwashers who worked nights and had to catch the early bus back out of the city to the first several stops that were too far for the local line. But Imogen had insisted on the trip and wouldn't let them put it off any longer. She had been reading about the vineyards in Médanos and had been telling them about it for weeks; and they had all decided to make a day of it. Chad wanted nothing to do with it—he hated to leave the city and the comfort of his own little world there. Sebastian had tried to convince Imogen that just he and she should go, but she had insisted Chad come along. They were engaged to be married after all. And so they stayed up drinking all night and were there with a bottle of wine when the ticket office opened before the sun was up. And they slept on the bus the entire way and only got off at a stop for a bottle of water because they could not yet stomach any food.

They'd had lunch in Bahía Blanca when the bus finally pulled in before noon because they were starving and could not resist the café across from the station. Imogen ate but then was sick in the toilet. Only more wine made her feel better. From there it was only another half hour by taxi to Médanos and the wineries there. They bought two cheap bottles from a man in town who wrapped them in brown paper and sold them a flimsy wine cork before they headed out into the green fields.

At a small farmhouse along the road, Sebastian had seen an old but functional bicycle leaning against a brick wall. It had no lock, and after inspecting it he'd decided it should accompany them, so he let Imogen ride it. Sebastian and Chad walked along with her. Imogen was laughing because they had already finished two bottles of wine at lunch, but Chad was not amused. He hadn't wanted to take the bike, but he had said nothing at the time.

They spent their day walking through the fields and along the dirt roads, taking turns with the bike, but mostly letting Imogen ride down whenever there were hills. They lay in the grass and slept in the sun and tried to eat the grapes that were sour and hard.

Now, with the sun down, they were not lost, but they were letting Chad be upset. No one spoke of the real reason he was mad. No one spoke of how Imogen and Sebastian had slipped away when Chad had fallen asleep, and how they had gone several rows down and kissed, and how Sebastian had wanted more but Imogen wouldn't let him. And they didn't speak about how Chad had called their names when he woke up and couldn't find them, and how they had run away and then came back along the road as if they had been on a walk. But Chad had seen them running away when he had called to them. No one spoke about that.

So now they were letting Chad be upset for a while. If either Sebastian or Imogen spoke, they knew he would only lash out more, and they wouldn't give him that. They had been with him too long and knew him too well. So instead they said nothing.

"God damn it, Im," Chad went on under his breath. "God damn it."

He went on like this for some time, raising his voice from time to time, and other times being nearly silent. It was when he got quiet that they knew he was really upset. But they had to just let him be.

Finally, once the sun was down and it was almost fully dark, Imogen silently picked up the bike and started walking it down the double-grooved road back toward the lighted house. Sebastian and Chad simply stood there and watched her go. Then they looked at each other, and then to the ground, and then they followed her.

They were silent walking up to the house—Imogen up front with the bike and Sebastian and Chad following her. As they approached, they felt the warmth of the house as it welcomed them. A man who had been working under the hood of an old truck waved to them as they came near.

"*Buenas noches*," he said. "Good evening."

"*Buenas noches*," Imogen replied. She was the only one of the three who spoke any decent Spanish.

The man smiled.

"We borrowed this bicycle," said Imogen. "I hope you do not mind."

"*Nada*," said the man. "I hope you found it useful. Did you enjoy your day?"

"*Sí*," said Imogen, "*muchas gracias.*"

The man took the bike, and they all stood in silence.

"How do we get back to town?" asked Imogen finally.

"Oh," said the man. "I would give you a ride in the truck, but I just removed the sparkplugs. I can have my wife call you a taxi from town."

"*Sí*," said Imogen. "A taxi will be fine. *Gracias.*"

The man left them for a moment and went inside the house.

They had made no plans. They had not made any real plans before they had set out on the bus. Maybe they would get a hotel room in Bahía Blanca. It was a big enough city. Sebastian had money. He always paid for everything. Imogen knew that's why Chad kept him around, because Chad was cheap and Sebastian paid for everything every chance he got. He had bought the bus tickets, he had bought the lunches, he had paid for the cab ride, and for the bottles of wine.

The three sat silently. The man came out and offered them some bread and cheese and wine that he brought from the house. He poured them each a full glass and told them about the wine and how his family had had this place for eight generations. A woman came out of the house and stood briefly at the door and waved hello to them, but she did not approach them. They ate in silence while only Imogen spoke to the man. Sebastian and Chad said nothing. Sebastian ate, Chad just drank the wine. Imogen and Sebastian just watched him without speaking and knew how it would be with him that night once they got to the hotel.

Twenty minutes later they all saw the lights of the taxi coming over the hill along the dirt road far in the distance. They all sat in silence as it came to a stop. It was an old woody green station wagon with a lighted sign on top. The driver got out and shook everyone's hand.

"Well," said the man, "I hope you three enjoy your evening."

"*Gracias,*" said Imogen. "*Usted también.*"

The man waved to them and watched them all the way as the red tail-lights of the cab went out of sight. Then he rolled the bike to a shed around the side of the house and leaned it against an inside wall. He went back and closed the hood of the truck. He would put in the new sparkplugs in the morning before he went into town for oil and a new belt for the tractor.

He went inside and found his wife at the sink humming a song he knew very well. He waited until she was finished rinsing some potatoes before he went to wash his hands. Then he took a dish towel and leaned over and kissed his wife on the cheek.

He and Alba had been married for forty-four years. Their children were now grown with children of their own.

None of the children would be taking over the winery. He sat in the chair at the head of the table and watched her heavy hips as she walked back and forth bringing dishes full of food to the table. He studied her—the way she walked, the thin but definite lines in her face, her thick but gray hair. She was no less beautiful today than when she was seventeen. But it was a different kind of beauty now. He smiled to himself and listened to her humming.

"Were those kids nice?" asked Alba.

"*Sí*," said the man. "Of course. They were very nice."

"*Sí?*"

"Yes," said the man. "They were in love."

"Really?" she asked. "Which ones?"

The man considered this for a moment. He laughed. "All of them," he said, smiling, nodding his head. "All three of them."

BROTHER OLLIE

The door to the coffee shop flew open with the arrival of two bundled figures that climbed inside and rushed to push the door closed against the first breaking cold of winter that now swirled high around the room. Everyone in the place looked toward the door and cringed until, after what seemed an eternal few seconds, the door was closed and the relative warmth and conversation slowly returned. Oliver distractedly watched the couple find a seat and dismantle their woolen armor before turning back to his plate of dry toast and runny eggs. The tired waitress across the counter who had just started her shift reached over and refilled his cup with coffee.

"S'more cream?" he mumbled as he played with the sugar packets between his rough fingers. The place had the feeling of overprotected warmth, as if the glass windows were walls of a fortress against a force unseen. Yet, as he still had on his coat and had been there for an hour, Oliver felt refreshed by the cool air that had come in and blown over his wind-burned face.

He had decided on the earlier train from Philadelphia—to take some time in the City, he told himself—but the biting cold and the awkwardness of carrying his suitcase with a handle that had broken on the train forced him into the subway and now into the diner a few blocks from his brother's apartment on the Upper West Side. There he would wait until five when, his brother told him, someone would be home to let him in. The newspaper in his hand was only a moderate distraction; the people and cars going by outside stole his attention, and he watched in the mirror high on the wall as his bundled subjects turned the corner and hurried down Broadway. He looked at his watch as the woman set the cream down in front of him.

"Gotta be somewhere?" she asked with a forced smile.

"Nah," he said, but it came out more like a grunt, and he shook his head to answer. Stirring his coffee, he realized he hadn't caught what time it was and looked at his watch again. "An hour and a half," he said to himself, and sat back heavily into his high-backed stool.

It was a chance at a job that brought him here. A friend he'd known from high school was setting him up with an ad agency that he worked for near the Park. They were looking for a new billboard salesman. Oliver was looking for anything that would get him out of this rut. This was the first chance he could take enough time off work from his regular job in Philly to make it up here without letting his boss find out. He had given an excuse about helping his mother move apartments. As he thought about this, he looked around the place and wondered how all these people could sit in a coffee shop in the middle of the day, and if he was the only one in the world who worked twelve-hour shifts.

A few more sips of his coffee and he managed to make it through another piece of toast and one or two of the articles from his paper, then he glanced back after staring around the room in the mirror and couldn't remember what he'd read. He reached down toward his feet and played with the handle of his luggage beneath his stool and saw that it could not be fixed, as the threads in the leather strap had torn through. He was getting warm and he took off his coat and put it in the only empty stool in the place that was next to him; and, after a few more minutes, he looked again at his watch and saw that it was nearly four and he would leave in an hour.

After three long buzzes up to the apartment and an awkward silence shared with a woman coming out of the building, he heard a scratchy voice coming back that he did not recognize.

"It's Oliver," he answered, and the door buzzed and he hurried to get through it and out of the stinging cold.

The stairs of the building were newly painted in a deep blue acrylic and had a daunting look as a glance upward reminded him of the number next to his brother's name by the door–802. He looked around for the elevator and found it just beyond the stairwell. "Rather hidden," he said aloud.

When he finally heard the deadbolt turn, he stood looking at a face he did not know. Must be the nanny, he thought, and introduced himself with a nod to the woman. She seemed not to speak any English, and he deciphered after a few short sentences that she was speaking Spanish and fully presumed that he spoke it as well. He did not. She quickly showed him to his room and left him to return to the baby he heard crying in another room. His room—what seemed to be a large empty closet that opened through a window onto a balcony—offered a small mattress on pine legs just raised above the floor, and seemed cozy enough. He set his cumbersome suitcase down next to the mattress and laid the coat over it. A few minutes later he settled himself outside against the rail of the balcony smoking a cigarette that he had wanted to smoke ever since entering the café.

There wasn't much to see there from the small, rusted iron balcony. Between a few buildings opposite him, he could make out a street and a sidewalk and a vacant park beyond. The cold of the air was still present, but the lack of wind there and the warmth from the cigarette made it tolerable. A bus passed on the street and echoed between the buildings toward him. The few people who moved about on the sidewalk made no sounds and seemed separated from him as if they were set to run on a mechanized track.

Oliver's brother Tom had received the call from Oliver a few days before at work because, Oliver said, he tried the house and no one there had answered. He wasn't even sure if the number worked anymore. So he had called the office and Tom took the call from his secretary.

"Sure, Ollie. You can stay at our place…as long as you need." As he said this, Tom winced at leaving the invitation open like that. But his brother assured him it would only be for a day or two while he was there for the interview. "We'll make sure there's room from you."

"You're sure I won't be in the way?" asked Oliver.

"Of course not. You're welcome any time."

Oliver was the oldest of four sons, and Tom was the second youngest. The family had not heard from Oliver in nearly a year.

Oliver heard someone step slowly out onto the balcony behind him but did not turn around. His brother Tom stepped up to the iron rail next to him and leaned over and looked out to where Oliver was looking. There was a long silence that acknowledged each other's presence.

"Just think," Oliver finally broke the silence, "if I get this job, we could be neighbors." He looked over at his brother and met his eyes for the first time in a long while. They both laughed uneasily.

Tom, still in his suit from work, leaned over and put a hand on his brother's shoulder. "I'd like that, Ollie," he said. "That would be really nice."

Oliver turned and leaned with his back against the rail again, lighting another cigarette.

"Those are gonna kill you, ya know," Tom laughed.

"That's what I'm hoping for." He watched the smoke from the match lift in the cold air and smelled its familiar phosphoric sting. That smell, mixed with the freshly lit tobacco and the cold winter air, was the smell he had grown to love most.

"We won't be here much longer, though," Tom interrupted Oliver watching the smoke curl away from his face.

"What's that?"

"If you move here, we won't be here much longer—in this apartment, I mean." His brother shifted and looked down over the rail. A cold gust of air came between the buildings and rushed over them. "With the baby here now, we're looking for a bigger place."

"Oh yeah? Where?" asked Oliver.

"Close to here. We're looking at a place two blocks up. Or maybe a place outside the City. There's not enough room anymore."

"How is it?" asked Oliver after a long breath from his cigarette. "…having your own family now?"

"Oh, it's great." Tom turned and leaned back like his brother. "Things are really good. Katie's good. The baby's good. Everything's really good."

Oliver looked up and blew the smoke high above him.

"So what's this interview you've got tomorrow?" Tom asked.

"It's at an ad agency. Friend set it up for me. You remember Joe Stanton."

"Yeah. Tall kid. Big ears."

"Yeah. He told me his boss is looking for a salesman for billboard space. Nice gig, if I can get it, he said. Paid on commission, though. Tiny salary, but really just commission."

"It'll be a nice change from working at the factory, then?"

Oliver thought about this for a while. "Sure will," he said. "But I've been at that factory three years now and there might be a shift supervisor spot opening soon. This old guy's fixin' to retire, on account of his health. Or just die right out."

"What's wrong with him?"

"He's just gettin' old."

Tom laughed. He felt the iron rail he was leaning on sway with his laughter, and he pulled some of his weight back from the edge.

Oliver turned and flicked his shortened cigarette over the rail and watched it fall with a glitter of burning ash.

"Hey, Tommy…," Oliver looked at his brother watching the cigarette fall. "…sorry I missed the wedding and everything. I was…"

"Ahh, no worries," said his brother. "I know you've been busy with work."

"I got the invitation. I tried to take off, but the plant manager said he'd fire me if I did. Too many people, not enough jobs. Gotta take what I can get and keep what I got."

"I understand, Ollie. It wasn't a big affair. There were only a few people there. We just had to get the damn thing done."

"Yeah, I know."

"Everyone was asking about you, though."

"Yeah? Like who?"

"Everyone. Hank and Amy. John Cassini. They just wanted to know what you were up to—how you were and everything."

"How big was Katie?"

Tom laughed. He thought back to the wedding and how funny it all really was. "She was about to burst!"

"I bet Ma was proud."

"We couldn't hide it. Katie was more than eight months pregnant. There was nothing we could do. Ma didn't care anyways. She just wanted a grandkid, you know. Now she has one. She's happy."

"Now maybe she'll get off my back then," said Oliver.

"Yeah. Maybe."

"Boy or girl?"

"He's a boy."

"What's the kid's name? You didn't name him after Pops, did you?"

"No," said Tom. "It's Antoine."

Oliver repeated the name slowly. "An-toine. An-toine." It felt nice to say it. It felt nice to be an uncle.

"Katie calls him Tony. I don't like it, though. I don't like the name Anthony. It reminds me of Cousin Tony, and I don't like that. I like Antoine better. She picked the name, of course. Family name, she said."

Oliver was still saying the name over and over softly with his lips.

"That's right. You haven't met him yet, have you?"

"No, not yet. I just heard him crying. I didn't want to get in the way."

"He's a good kid," said Tom. "Doesn't do much yet. Just eats and sleeps and cries a lot. Poops all the time. We'll go see him in a minute."

Tom had heard his wife come home and heard her talking to the nanny in the kitchen in simple Spanish. He knew that dinner would be ready soon, but he liked being out here talking to his brother. It had been such a long time.

After dinner, Oliver made his way into a chair in the living room to watch television while Tom and Katie finished cleaning up. He had offered to help, but they said he was a guest there and wouldn't let him touch a thing. They had placed Antoine in his crib next to him, and he passed his attention to the kid during commercials. His back molar that had been bothering him on the train started aching again, and he ran his tongue over it and over the gums that ached. It was only getting worse.

"Don't grow up, kid," he said to Antoine. "It doesn't get any easier. Only gets hard and stays that way."

Over the sound of the television, the clanging of dishes and conversation from the kitchen caught his attention. What he first heard as a low murmur had risen to an audible conversation between Katie and Tom. He tried not to listen, but couldn't help it.

"…So you're mad at me then?" he heard his brother say.

"No."

"There's something wrong. He's my brother, Kat."

"Did you give him any money?"

Tom didn't say anything.

"How much did you give him?"

"Just a few dollars. Just to help him out."

"He's always asking for money, and you always give in. We need that money!"

"But he always pays it back."

"That's not the point. We need that money for Tony. You can't let him get over on you like that all the time." The conversation rose over the television.

"I know…it's just that…"

The baby started to cry and the two stopped talking. Oliver reached over quickly and got the baby's attention and quieted him. The talking in the kitchen resumed after a few seconds of silence, this time back to a murmur.

"Look," said Tom, "he just needs a little help to get back on his feet." There was a pause where no one spoke. Tom continued. "It's gonna happen for him."

"Yeah, but when?"

There was no answer.

The morning came after a long night of lying awake, staring at the ceiling, concluded by an hour or so of half-sleep that left Oliver feeling tired all day. Oliver thumbed the money his brother had given him and wondered if he could give it back before he left, but he needed to get the subway to Lexington and still hadn't bought his train ticket back out of the City. He would give it back as soon as he could, with a little extra. As he placed the money back in his wallet, his fingers passed over a worn picture of his first wife that he tried not to look at anymore. Still, he couldn't take it out of the wallet completely.

The suit he wore was not the suit he had brought with him. His brother had passed by as he was getting dressed that morning and had let him borrow one of his own suits that might make a better impression. Oliver was a little heavier than his brother, and his arms were a little longer, but if he kept his shoulders back it didn't look bad. Not bad at all.

Oliver looked at his watch and it was ten o'clock now. The interview was at one. Tom and Katie had left early for work, and the nanny had come by at seven to take the baby for the day. Oliver was left alone in the apartment. He walked from room to room, not wanting to sit down and wrinkle the suit pants. Every reflection he passed, he caught himself and straightened his tie or pushed his hair back from his forehead. In the living room, on a shelf chest-high, sat a group of wedding pictures he had not noticed the night before. Everyone looked so nice in their dresses and suits, Oliver thought, and he was mad at himself for not being there and for not talking to his family for so long. It wasn't work that had kept him from going to the wedding—it had been something inside him that he couldn't face yet. He looked at a picture of Katie and saw that she really didn't look that pregnant. The photographer had done a good job with that. He looked at his watch again and only ten minutes had passed. His legs were getting tired of standing. Finally, he went and turned on the television and sat carefully down in the chair so as not to wrinkle his pants. He would leave at noon with plenty of time to make it to Lexington.

When Oliver arrived back at the apartment that evening, Katie was already home with the nanny cooking dinner. The television was on in the kitchen, entertaining the baby. He wanted to get up to his room quietly so that no one would notice.

"Tom…is that you?" Katie called from the kitchen.

Oliver rounded the hall corner and smelled dinner. As he took another step, Katie appeared before him.

"Oh, hi, Oliver. I thought it was Tom."

Oliver nodded. There was an awkward exchange between them where no one said anything.

"Dinner should be ready by seven," she said, then disappeared into the kitchen.

"Thanks," said Oliver. He was glad she had not asked how the interview went.

Oliver made it into his room and took his coat off. Before he undressed, he went to his luggage and pulled out his checkbook and made his way back to the kitchen. He reached out an envelope to Katie who had her hands deep in a bowl of dough.

"This is for Tom," he said.

Katie nodded to the counter. "Just put it over there and I'll make sure he gets it."

Oliver hesitated. "There's a check in there for him."

Katie looked at him. He caught a weak smile on her face, and also a light blush. She was a very pretty woman. He had never really spoken to her before.

"I was going to drop it in the mail, but…I'll just leave it here."

"Oh. Thank you, Oliver. I'll let him know."

Oliver turned to walk out, then caught himself. "If you could tell Tommy to call me before he cashes it, that would be good."

Katie nodded to him and turned back to kneading the dough.

On the balcony, Oliver pulled out a fresh pack of cigarettes he had bought in the subway station and lit one in his lips. Today was warmer than yesterday, and a light breeze made its way through the buildings to him. Oliver looked out at the street he had seen yesterday and narrowed his eyes; through the trees that had lost all their leaves he noticed that he could see the Hudson. After his second cigarette, he heard Tom come home and talk to his wife and then to Antoine.

"Where is Oliver?" Tom asked.

"I don't know. He came in, but I think he went to his room."

In a few minutes, Tom emerged and joined his brother on the balcony. As before, there was a long silence before anyone spoke. Finally, Tom cleared his throat.

"So...how'd it go?"

Oliver was dreading the question. There was only silence. The silence told Tom how it went.

Tom sighed. "That bad, huh?"

Oliver flicked the cigarette from the balcony. "Oh, not that bad. I don't have any sales experience, but they said they'd give me a call to let me know. I think it went all right."

Tom nodded. "Well, like you said, Ollie, maybe we'll be neighbors soon."

Oliver smiled and looked over at his brother. He looked to see if he could tell that he was lying—to see if he could tell that Oliver had not even gone up the elevator to the interview, but instead had sat for an hour in the lobby of the building watching the people walk by—watching the clock on the wall as the interview time slowly came and then went. Another half hour had passed. Around two o'clock he'd had trouble keeping his eyes open, and when he leaned over and put his head on the armrest the concierge came over and asked him if he were waiting for someone. He said yes and then felt thirsty and left to find a place for a drink to pass the rest of the afternoon.

There was another long pause. Oliver pulled out another cigarette.

"Do you have one for me?" asked Tom.

"A cigarette?"

"Yeah."

"You don't smoke."

"Sure I do…every now and then." He said this as if trying to convince himself. Oliver heard it in his voice.

Oliver handed him a cigarette and lit it for him. Tom held back a cough.

"You know," said Oliver, "she'll smell it on you."

"Who? Katie?" He looked at his brother. "I can smoke if I want to."

"Sure you can, Tommy."

The two laughed, an occasion that Tom used to clear his lungs.

Oliver smiled at his brother. "You can blame the smell on me if you want."

Tom nodded with a smile. "Thanks."

Oliver lay awake as he had the night before, staring at the thin cracks in the plaster ceiling and listening to the clock on the wall. His watch had a similar tick, and he listened to the two beats move in and out of synch and wondered which one was fast and which was slow.

He lay in his own suit on top of the mattress and bare pillow ready to leave for the train; the sheets and pillow case lay folded neatly on top of the wood chest next to him. He had packed already and had noticed that someone had sewn the handle on his suitcase so that he could carry it again. The stitching was a little rough, but it was strong and would hold. He wondered whether the nanny or Katie had done it.

Another hour passed, and the incessant ticking of the clock and his watch had grown unbearable. That, and the pain from his molar, made it impossible to sleep, and he rolled off the mattress and grabbed his suitcase and stood silently at the door before turning off the light. A few silent steps down the hall, he passed Antoine's room. The floor creaked slightly, and he heard the baby stir. He stopped and put a hand on the door to the room as if he wanted to say something to him. It creaked a little, and he pulled back. He listened for a moment, but the baby didn't start to cry.

In the kitchen, he saw the envelope still on the counter and placed the spare key they had given him next to it. Then he opened the apartment door slowly so as not to make any noise, then made sure the door would lock when he shut it.

Down below, he stepped out into the dark street and into the smell of the air and the sounds of the pigeons cooing in the cool winter morning. It was cold, but it wasn't windy, and there was a certain sereneness about being awake in the City before anyone else. Any sounds were far off, as if they were part of the natural world. He looked at his watch. He would walk to the station instead of catching a cab or the subway. The first train back to Philadelphia wouldn't leave for another three hours.

DOWN IN THE KEYS

The first day was the hardest for all of us. By the end of the first day, there were muscles aching we didn't even know we had. My old man had the hardest time, of course. That's because he's got thirty years on us. And the chafing got him the worst, too. But the aching and the chafing, it was nothing a little rum that evening couldn't help. I didn't mind hanging back with my old man a little. I liked being with him. Jake stayed in front. We all knew he would. We knew he had to show off or something. That's just the way it was. We didn't mind. By the end of the second day we were all getting the hang of it and taking it easy now and then and liking it even more, and we were all glad we had made the trip together.

We'd started up near Key Largo. That was where we put the kayaks in, up in the mangrove cuts where we spent the first morning going around the island and through the narrow channels. The mangroves grew in so close some places you had to unscrew your paddle at the middle and row it like a canoe. That was our favorite part, except we knew Jake wanted to get moving. We had six miles we had to cover that first day, and it wasn't getting any shorter after that.

Our first stop was just a half mile down, set off away from the road that ran down all the way to Key West. It was an old white settlement that had been overrun by Indians back in the eighteen hundreds or something, and there wasn't much left of it but a few coral shell foundations and cisterns for getting water. There were a few of these places scattered all the way down the Keys. We didn't stay long. We ran our kayaks up on the sand and walked across the island and back in twenty minutes or so. The sun was hot and only getting hotter, and we wanted to stay on the water early and get the paddling done as early as we could. We set out again just before noon and ate our sandwiches and drank our warm beers as we paddled, and we just kept along the islands out of the wind if we could between the wide channels. And then we knew it was all ahead of us now.

The first night we camped up under the mangroves and tried the best we could with our gear, but it had been a long time since we'd all camped together—fifteen years maybe—and there was a lot that came back to us later as the week went on. In the warmth of the muggy night we all had trouble sleeping with the mosquitoes whining around us and the cars going down the islands on the road a hundred yards away. But the beer and the rum made us feel good, and my old man was out right away because you could hear him breathing that way, and I just lay awake thinking how good it was we could all make the trip. I could hear Jake and Casey talking in the tent next to us. Jake was my younger brother. But he was grown now, too. He was twenty-four and had a wife and a kid on the way. We were all grown now. Casey wasn't our brother, but he looked a lot like it. We used to kid him and tell him he was our brother but that we'd sold him away because we couldn't afford to feed him anymore—he ate too much. When he was young that made him cry, but not anymore. Now it just made us all laugh.

The second day on the water was a pretty good day. We made better time because we all wanted to get the paddling done early, and we started out when the sun was coming up and got to the next stop just after noon. For breakfast we ate cereal out of plastic bowls because it was easy and we didn't want to make a big deal about it like we did supper the night before. We opened a can of condensed milk and poured it over the cereal. It was better than nothing. I had made the packing list, and I wasn't sure how that would turn out, but nobody complained. I had also done the map and chosen our stopping points where we would camp, and when we reached the spot the second day so early I studied the map for ten minutes because there was no way we could have made it so fast. But Jake was sure, and there was no point arguing. We had three more days of good solid paddling ahead of us, so we would get there eventually. As Casey and Jake and the old man went swimming and fishing in the clear green water between the mangrove islands, I walked up to the two-lane road and found a sign and saw that we had stopped a mile short. That put us maybe a half hour behind, but it didn't matter too much because I had left an extra day at the end of the trip in case we got behind.

Up near the road it felt strange seeing civilization again. All I saw was the road and a gas station and a few cars going by, but when you're on the water for two days straight and all you see is the water and the islands and the bridges in the distance, you see everything differently. It was strange to feel the ground beneath me, too, because it wasn't moving like when you were in the boat, and it felt strange standing there on the hard packed shell dirt.

All the gear we had piled on the fronts and backs of the kayaks under the mesh that held everything in place. After the first day, we took our life vests off because they were getting us pretty bad under the arms, so we tied them over our food packs to keep the sun off them. That made the rowing easier, but we had more to cover with the sun lotion, so we ran out pretty quick because we had to put it on every hour. We all had big hats on, too, that kept the sun off our faces, and those worked pretty well except when Casey's blew off and we had to cut a hole in it and tie a string through it around his neck so he wouldn't lose it anymore.

The third day was pretty bad because we had the extra mile to make up and because the sun was pretty awful and there wasn't any wind to cool things off. Just the heat and the sun and no wind. We stopped in a run-down marina that looked like it had been abandoned in the seventies and found a bait shop that was open and bought some more sun lotion and a twelve-pack of beers that were cold. And we killed those off just before lunch because we still had a ways to go. The good thing was that the wind was down, so there weren't any waves except between the islands in the channels as the tide changed, and we made good time. Jake still stayed in front and I stayed back near our dad, and Casey hung out somewhere in between. My dad was pretty happy seeing us all there. He wasn't in any rush to get anywhere, and I think he could have been out front if he wanted to. I think he was just happy seeing us all there together. When we broke for lunch by running our bows onto a sandy mangrove island that gave us some shade, we all decided that we would find a motel that night near the water where we could tie up our kayaks instead of camping. After two nights in the tents, we were pretty eaten up by mosquitoes and covered in dried salt, and I think we all just wanted a shower and a nice bed to sleep in. We made it to the stopping point at about four-thirty, and the map showed a little town on an island about a half mile up, so we decided to keep going.

With the kayaks tied up safe on the dock, we all checked into the motel that was painted bright yellow and green and got hot showers and felt better. We all felt a little sick from the sun and being on the land and not feeling things move beneath us, so we found a bar down the road and got a few beers and dinner and listened to a radio and talked to a few of the people at the bar. There was a couple in their fifties from Tennessee, and they were burnt red as can be. It hurt just looking at their faces. Among us, Casey was the most burnt because he didn't put on as much lotion, but the rest of us hardly showed any sun at all, even after three days with the sun above us and the light bouncing up off the water. We didn't want to get burned. We knew that would ruin the trip for us. We knew sunburns all too well.

The beds that night felt incredible after our sleeping bags. It was a small motel, so each of the rooms only had one bed, but it wasn't any less comfortable than sleeping in the tents. I stayed with Casey, and my dad and Jake stayed in the other room, but we all stayed up late drinking more than we should have with the couple from Tennessee and a few other people at the bar. And we all knew the next morning that the day was going to be rough. But it wasn't as bad as we'd thought. After we had breakfast our stomachs felt better, and the day went pretty well up until the end. The tide was low in the morning and running strong and there were parts on the west side of the islands where the water was so clear and shallow that you could walk over the sand in just a few inches of water, but we made better time by paddling it. Jake got out and walked for a bit, but the sand shifted under his feet and it was better in the boats. There were tarpon rolling where the water got deeper over the sand, and we stayed close to them for a good half hour and followed them until they stopped rolling and gulping anymore, and all we could see were their silvery bodies moving away from us through the clear water. We had a fishing pole, but we only had a spinner, and they wouldn't take it even though we threw it right in the middle of them. They didn't seem to pay any attention to it at all. Up near the mangroves when we pulled into the shade we sometimes came up on small nurse sharks lying in the sun that skirted away when we came up. But sometimes you could get close enough to some to reach out your paddle and touch them, and they moved away slowly sometimes. And then there were the thousands of fiddler crabs that covered the sand on some of the islands and moved in big red masses when you pulled up near them. Casey liked chasing them back and forth. He never caught one.

We came upon an old mangrove island where the road down to Key West once passed through, but it was all abandoned now because the bridge took the road straighter now away from the island. We got out and walked around and studied the broken asphalt with its painted lines and how everything had grown over with time, and we half expected to see someone or something come out at us—we didn't know what—but nothing ever came.

Toward the end of the day the wind came up, and when we pulled up for camp we knew it would storm. There was lightning far off under the dark clouds and we didn't want to be on the water when the wall of rain hit. When it did finally come we felt the wind change and the air get cold and knew it wasn't just a quick storm that would pass over us. All that night the wind blew and the gray clouds threw down rain, and we knew it would be rough the next day if we could get on the water at all. In the night, the tents blew around us and came in on us no matter how hard we staked them down or tied them to the mangroves, and all we could do was just huddle in our wet sleeping bags and not sleep and try to stay warm and just wait for it all to pass over. In the morning it was all pretty wet and the camp was a mess, but the storm offered us no relief and we made breakfast in the lee of a big group of mangroves and tried to stay warm and dry the best we could. It was not a true cold because it was still summer, but it was the kind of cold that comes with the summer storms and hits you hardest because you've been in the sun for the better part of a week, and your body just takes it differently. We looked at the sky and talked about it and knew it would only get worse, so we stayed in camp that day inside our tents and watched the gray chop of the water, and that only got worse, too. We did our best to bear it through the night, but I'm sure none of us got any sleep with the wind and the rain not having let up, and we all wished we were back in the motel or anywhere but here. And on the morning of the next day it didn't look any better, and we knew we wouldn't make the last day on the water. We were all hoping to get to Crawl Key on Marathon, and we had even given ourselves an extra day just in case, and we finally decided and sent Jake up to the road to catch a ride the last six miles down to Marathon where we had left one of the trucks. He came back in the rain, and we tied down the kayaks and the rest of our gear in the bed the best we could and rode warm but silent back up to Key Largo with the rain coming down against the foggy windshield.

We were all pretty sorry we didn't get to finish the trip the way we wanted to, and we were all pretty quiet in the two trucks heading back up from Key Largo to Miami. But we knew things like that could happen in the summer-time, and we stopped at a hotel there for the night because we had to catch our flights out the next day. We had a good shower and a meal and a few beers and some glasses of rum and agreed the trip was good and that it wasn't ruined by the storm.

The next morning it was a Sunday and the weather had all blown over and we all wanted to stay just a little longer. But we had to catch our planes, and my old man still had to drive back home to Tampa with the kayaks loaded in the back of his truck. We never did take another trip like that, the four of us, but we always talked about it anytime any of us were together or talked on the phone. That was the best part of it—that we could talk about it so much afterwards—because we didn't talk about it much while we were down there in the islands. And it was worth it to know that sometimes it really is as good as you remember it, when we were younger and our lives didn't get in the way.

THE LONG WAY
BACK HOME

Greyhound makes twenty-two stops between San Fran and Bozeman. Transfer at Reno, Salt Lake, and Butte, then straight on east to Gallatin County. Just over a day and a half if you take it all at once.

At Rexburg in Idaho we stop for thirty so people can get outside and eat somethin'. Driver needs gas anyway, and across from the station there's a little diner. It's almost midnight. Inside I get a half decent cup of coffee, for somethin' to do. First one of the trip. Funny thing drinkin' coffee at midnight.

"Rain's let up," someone says at the counter. Man next to him from the bus nods. He's been asleep since Salt

Lake. Slept through the whole damn thing. Waitress tells me there's no charge for the coffee. Usually fifty cents. I can tell she used to be pretty before life beat it out of her. Lines across her face and hair dyed fire red with the roots turned gray. I set down a dollar and she smiles at me as I walk out. Shame lettin' a woman like that go to hell.

Back on the bus headin' west toward Highway 15 a Mexican family gets on and I don't have the open seat next to me anymore. Don't mind, really. Only got five stops left 'til Butte. Three hours. We'll get into Butte at three in the mornin'.

Nevermind hitchhikin'. If you've got someplace to be you never know where you'll end up because they're not goin' your way, or if you'll ever get there at all, these crazies that pick up hitchhikers now. Might as well pay the fare and get there straightaway. Bus ain't so bad. Not if you don't mind sittin' so long. And me with my knees pressin' up against the seat in front of me. Nope, just want to get back home now. California didn't work out. Not for me. They all said it wouldn't when I left, and they were right. Wished me luck anyways, and my old man even sent me off with a few bucks. But you've got high hopes and want to get out of what's been laid out before you, and maybe you just want to take a chance of your own and try to make somethin' of it.

But it didn't work out. Not for me.

'Bout an hour out of Lima near Dillon, with the rain comin' back on, one of the back left tires goes out and the driver stops to radio for service. I look at my watch and it's two in the mornin'. Couldn't sleep. After about five minutes of waitin' the Mexican next to me and I get up and ask the driver where the spare is, and another ten minutes we're back on the road with him and me soaked through and covered thick in brake dust. But we don't mind much because we'd've been there an hour just sittin'. No need for that. The Mexican didn't speak the whole time, but we've both changed enough tires we didn't need to say nothin'.

That's what I'm good at. Gettin' dirty and changin' tires. Diggin' ditches, layin' fence posts, bailin' hay. Maybe that's good enough. Maybe it's got to be.

Soaked through and back on our way, the road is dead straight for a few miles and I nod off against the glass. The heater near the window keeps me warm and I half wake up every time we slow or hit a bump. Bus stops at Melrose and I wake up and think it's Butte or that I missed my stop. But the sign says Melrose and I keep myself awake now because we're less than an hour out. Once we hit Butte at three in the mornin' I've got a transfer just after noon that'll take me to Bozeman. Solid nine hours of waitin'. Only bus that day to Bozeman. Not sure how I'll keep myself busy. But once I get to Bozeman I'll get off there and try to catch a ride the last twenty miles to the Ranch. Everyone knows the Paxton Ranch. It's right up Highway 86. I can trust these people for a ride. They're my people. No matter how much I didn't want them to be when I left.

Bus finally pulls into a parking lot in Butte and lets me off in the rain and the darkness. I'm the only one gets off. I run over to the building with my bag to stay dry, but the door's locked. Nothin' but a soda machine outside. Ten minutes later the rain's no better so I walk to the other side of the building under the awning to see if there's another door. No door. No lights on inside.

After a half hour of sittin' the rain's let up just a little and there's even a break in the clouds where you can see a few stars against the black sky. I walk south to find a gas station through the orange glow of the few street lights. Orange all around. Inside I find the bathroom and mop up my hair and clothes with cheap brown paper towels in the warmth. Then I hang around for a while inside just to stay dry, stayin' outside of view of the guy behind the counter. Try to warm up a bit. But I'm the only one in there that early in the mornin'. I buy a cup of stale coffee in a paper cup for fifty cents and head back outside. Rain's stopped. Maybe there's hope just yet.

A block and a half away I find another gas station with a concrete wall to lean against. No more rain, but I get a place under the awning just to be sure. I sit on the sidewalk there and just huddle over and try to fall asleep with my bag under my knees. Nothin' to do but wait. Bus doesn't leave until after noon. I look at my watch. More'n eight hours left to wait.

It must be a few hours later and the sun wakes me up. My body's cold—chilled right through. And I've been shiverin' in my sleep. Didn't really sleep much, just dazed and dead tired from not sleepin' on the bus. Crazy thing the sun comin' up with the big sky above. Woke me right up, and I was tired as hell. I can barely move my body, and I'm damp and freezin', and I have to take a piss, bad.

So the sun's up and I feel like gettin' a jelly doughnut and some coffee. The blacker the better. I walk into the gas station, shiverin' cold. Sun's up now, so there's a few folks fillin' up or inside gettin' stale coffee. Warmer inside than where I was. And the piss is the best feelin' I've had in days.

Half an hour later I'm on the sidewalk outside again with my second coffee. I don't want to overstay my welcome with the guy inside. Plan on hangin' out here most of the day until my next bus to Bozeman, but the only place to sit is outside on the cold concrete.

Then, I think I'm imaginin' it, but I see a red Ford truck outside. Looks damn familiar. Looks like trucks I know. There's a decal on the passenger door. Yellow. Paxton Ranch, it says. Bright sun comin' up between two mountain peaks. Damn, I think to myself. Damn. Didn't expect to see that here. I'm nowhere near the Ranch yet.

I stand there a few minutes wonderin' who's drivin'.

A lady walks out, maybe younger'n me, maybe a bit older. She comes out with a big steamin' coffee and a brown paper bag with somethin' in it. I'm standin' near the truck, close enough to catch whoever's drivin'. Just might snag a ride.

I don't mean to talk to her, but she glances over at me.

"Hey, lady," I say, half under my breath, hopin' she won't hear me.

It's started sprinklin' again, and I duck back under the awning real quick.

She turns around toward me, but in the rain she speeds up towards the truck and gets in. Pretty enough girl. Tall and thin. Faded jeans and a green flannel shirt. 'Bout my age, from what I could tell.

"Hey, lady," I call again when she's inside. She's got the windows rolled up, so I run over and knock on the passenger window with the rain comin' down harder.

"Yeah?" she shouts with the window rollin' down.

"Hey, lady. You comin' from Paxton Ranch?"

"Yeah," she shouts.

"Well, look," I say. "I'm Hank. Hank Paxton. Roger Paxton's son."

She looks at me for a second, studyin' my face.

"Yeah?" she says. "So?"

I just stand there in the cold and the rain and shake my head.

"So," I say, "maybe you could take me with you, save me the bus trip."

She hesitates for a second. Nothin' I can do but stand there and get wet. But she sees me gettin' wet and waves me in without a word.

I get in and set my bag on the floor and the cup of coffee in the holder and slam the door. The cab is warm, and the seat is dry. More'n I could've asked for. I'm gonna soak it though.

"Sorry about the wet clothes," I say.

She looks at me for a second. "Cassie," she says.

"Huh?"

"I'm Cassie," she repeats.

"Hank," I say, but I'd already said that.

She starts backin' out, and the rain comes on again, harder this time. Real hard. Can barely see out the windows.

"Where you comin' from?" she asks, flippin' on the wipers.

"San Fran," I say. "California."

"California?"

"Yeah, California."

She nods.

"When d'you get in?"

"I don't know. Three. Three this mornin'."

"Yeah? Bus?"

"Yeah, three this mornin'."

"You tired then?"

"Nah," I say. "Not tired at all." But I just about can't keep my eyes open, even with the coffee.

"Ok. Well you just sit back for a bit. It'll be two hours before we get back."

"Yeah, I know," I say. But I didn't mean to make it sound rude.

"Maybe three, if there're tractors on the road."

"All right," I say again. "Thank ya. Real nice of ya."

I look at her, and I know right away my old man's shackin' up with this girl. She's 'bout my age. Can't be much older. But damn sure he's shackin' up with her. My ma left us when I was fourteen for the bank manager who held our mortgage in Bozeman. They went off to Chicago together, and we never heard from her since.

And here I am comin' home. Comin' home to take my rightful place next to Roger Paxton of the Paxton Steer Ranch. Someithin' I never wanted. I don't have the business mind my old man has. Just wanted to get dirty and sweat for a buck and then get drunk every night. Good life. No, this isn't what I wanted. My old man bought this land when he was twenty. Saved up enough workin' jobs in school, and bought a few acres at the edge of the Chapman acreage. Then grew it every chance he got, always on credit. But he's done all right for himself. Owns it outright now.

"Why you all the way out here?" I ask her. Bozeman is the next big town next to the Ranch, and we rarely ever made it out to Butte.

"Welding materials," she points with her thumb to the bed of the truck. "Aluminum wire and argon. All out in Bozeman. Gotta come here for it."

"Yeah," is all I say.

With the heat on and the windshield foggin' up, I can start to smell my clothes. Same clothes for two days without a change. She's bound to smell me, and I think about sayin' somethin' first, but I don't say nothin'.

Well maybe I didn't know it, but I must've been tired as hell, because maybe two and a half hours later I wake up with the bump of the truck goin' from the asphalt to gravel and I see we're pullin' up to the gate on Highway 86 and she's laughin' at me when I start awake.

I shake my head, tryin' to figure it all out.

"What?" I ask. I don't know if she said somethin' to me or not.

"Nothin'" she says, laughin'.

"Sorry, was I asleep?"

"Nah," she says, but she laughs at me anyway.

I must've fallen asleep right away. Haven't slept decent in nearly two days. I just feel wrung out.

So, there it is. Paxton Ranch. And here I am Hank Paxton, son of Roger Paxton, comin' back home. I picture us drivin' up to the house and parkin'. I picture the dogs. Toby and Jinx will run out and greet me, the way they always did whenever I drove in. That is, if Jinx is still alive. She was gettin' kinda old when I left. And I picture her pissin' all over the way she always did. Even when she was young. Couldn't hold her piss in when she saw me. And then I see my old man standin' in the doorway. Seein' me come home like this—couldn't make it on my own in California. I immediately shrink in my seat and regret the whole damn thing.

"Shit!" I say under my breath. But she hears me and looks over.

We ride on for another few seconds.

"Hey look," I say to the girl, "d'you mind stoppin' the truck?"

"Sure," she says, and she rolls to a stop right there with the last few bumps still rockin' us.

I don't move for a second, and she just looks over at me.

"Maybe I..." I start sayin', but I stop. Maybe I'm not ready to go back yet, I think to myself. Maybe not yet. But I don't say any of this to her, and I just keep it to myself. I think for a minute.

"Huh?" she says.

I reach down and grab my bag from between my feet. The floor down there is warm where the vent is blowin' hot air. I grab the door handle and crack the door. I turn back to her.

"Look," I say. "You mind not tellin' anyone?" I ask. "You know, don't tell the old man or anythin'?"

She looks at me, confused, but then a moment later she gets it. Without a word she nods to me. I think she understands. I think she knows what I'm gettin' at.

A few moments later I'm standin' outside the truck and the door is shut. It's not rainin', but there's a cool little drizzle comin' down. Mornin' clouds burnin' off. She reaches across and rolls the window down.

"You'll be all right?" she asks me.

"Sure," I say. "I'll be fine."

She nods. "Good luck, then. Maybe we'll see you again sometime. Hopefully soon."

"Maybe," I say. "Thank you much. For the ride."

Then, without rollin' the window up she starts movin' off toward the Ranch. And before long she's almost out of sight up the hard-packed road leadin' up to the house.

So there I am. A thousand miles on the bus, and I'm not more'n a few hundred yards from the house where I grew up. That's where I was headed. But that last quarter mile is the hardest part. I could walk it in a few minutes, but that ain't where I'm headed now. Not anymore.

I turn and walk back out to the main paved road. I look both ways. I'll head south on 86 back toward Bozeman and catch a tractor or a truck on the way. Who knows where I'll end up. Not here, though. Not yet. Gotta get far enough away so no one knows me, but then there'll be work anywhere I look. Diggin' ditches, layin' fence posts, bailin' hay. That's good enough for me. It's gonna have to be. For now.

KASIA

The dry, heavy breathing of the man filled the dark and otherwise soundless room. Thin curtains, nailed to the window frame, kept out what light they could, but they were not nearly enough—the day still crept through. A small room, surrounded in thin wood planks that weathered nails held impossibly together. There was no furniture except the bed on which the old man lay almost unmoving over a thin, wooden frame. The breathing was steady, coarse, low, defeated. Weakened by decades of strenuous toil. Within it, the ache the man had felt so long. Darkness swelling, melodic breathing. A plane of thin orange light sliced through the dusty air. The room consumed by the dank stench of urine and rotting wood.

From outside the thin, cracked door came a strained voice. "*Dziadek*," a woman whispered uneasily. "Grandfather," she said. There was no answer. She spoke again. "Grandfather, will you eat?"

Through the door, the woman heard the man's forced but steady breathing. Shifting the child nursing at her breast she placed a hand against the door with a heavy sigh, pushing until she could just peer inside. On the bed, the dark, massive silhouette, rising and falling imperceptibly with the sound that came with great effort. The narrow plane of light splitting the tear at the edge of the curtain flashed down sharply to the floor and cut the room in half. She stood for a moment to let her eyes adjust, listening, watching thousands of white specks float through the beam of light, trying to make out the heavy outline of the old man in the dark. She said nothing. There was only the great silence through which heavy breaths flowed and ceased and flowed again; then, the creak of the door as she left the room.

"Is he awake?" asked the man sitting on a hand-turned wooden stool at the head of a rough oak table, idly running the blade of his pocketknife flat across its grains. The planks of the table had been nailed into place not a week before, and a cool dampness still could be felt along the underside. Two boys sat quietly next to the man, watching him, watching their father turn the blade with a flash from the sun on each methodical stroke. The woman, coming to the sink with the nursing child held against her with one arm so that both hands were free, said nothing and shook her head no. The man did not see her but heard her silence and knew his own father lying in the next room was not awake. His eyes were fixed on the blade as it moved, on the blade and on the shiny smoothness it left on the surface of the wood. The woman reached into the sink and gathered up a handful of vegetable scraps and threw them out the window among a cluster of chickens scratching in the yard that rose up with a whirl of feathers and shrieks. Then, seeing their bounty before them, they threw themselves at it, pecking and screeching at each other for their proper share. The golden light of the afternoon sun shone through the window over the woman's face and made her look, if only for an instant, not so entirely tired, but almost youthful.

"Where's your sister?" she asked the boys behind her. The younger of the two boys had his forearm up to his face and was licking the back of it. "What are you doing?" she asked him as she looked over her shoulder.

"It's salty," the boy said innocently.

"Stop that! Where is your sister?"

The two looked at each other without speaking and then back at their mother.

"Go and get your sister," she said without looking at them, "or we don't eat."

The younger boy hesitated for a few moments and then stood up heavily, knowing it was his duty in the presence of his older brother, and walked outside the house, kicking at the chickens that scattered and then quickly regrouped. "Kasia!" he called loudly with his hands in front of his face before listening quietly for a response. There was no answer. He walked back into the kitchen through the open door, kicking again at the chickens as he returned, nearly striking one. "She's not there," he said as he moved to the table to sit back down.

With a quick motion that he didn't even see, the mother crossed the room from where she stood and grabbed her son by the shoulder with a rough hand and walked him back to the door. The child nursing at her breast was undisturbed. "Go and find her!" she said sternly, pushing him out with none of the tenderness that mothers are known to show their children. The older brother laughed at this, but a sharp look from his father silenced him instantly.

Outside, the growing cluster of chickens on the hard packed dirt broke apart into a flurry of cackles and feathers as the boy raced through them into the open yard. He kicked at one of them, a white one with patches of black feathers, and chased it for a moment until it flew up against the wood pile and scrambled away dazed. Behind him, the others had already regrouped and were pecking furiously at the scraps, scratching their feet in the dry dirt. He picked up a rock and threw it back at them. A moment later, he stood at the edge of an expansive field of wheat that seemed to have no end and paused to call out for his sister. "Kasia!" he yelled. "Dinner!" Again, there was no response. He listened for half a minute but heard nothing except the chickens and the wind blowing over the grain. He listened a moment longer, but there was nothing. A glance back at the house showed his mother looking severely at him through the window. Any sign of her youth had disappeared from her face. The boy rolled his eyes to himself and reluctantly threw his weight down the path among the thin stalks of grain, running and stopping to call out several times more.

Far out along a narrow stream at the edge of a high wooded break in the plain, beyond the winding rows of golden wheat and the field where the village's cattle grazed, two girls sat lazily in the warmth of the late summer sun. The long blonde hair of one of the girls lay spread among the grass as she stared at the sky above, her eyes half closed in a dreary daydream, watching the delicate clouds pass overhead. In her fingers, she played with a small carved wooden angel tied with a coarse string around her neck—a gift from a grandmother long passed. The other girl lay next to her, turning through the worn pages of a book she had read many times before. It was the only book she owned. A few steps away, a third girl, her dark hair cut short like a boy's, stood up to her knees in the gurgling water of the stream, making her way cautiously among the round, worn rocks with a fishing pole in her hand. The pole was nothing more than a bowed stick with a thin thread line and a hook her father had made from the rim of a can. The sound of the insects buzzing and the rippling water from the running stream hung in the air over them. In the summer, with little work to do on the farm until harvest, many days passed together this way for the girls in a satisfying blur.

One of the girls, the one who had been reading, picked up her eyes from the page and listened into the distance. "Kasia…" she said.

Kasia, whose eyes had been fixed high upon the clouds trying to spot an angel in them that resembled her necklace, took a moment to come back to reality and absently looked over at her. "Uh huh?"

"I thought I heard someone calling."

The two girls picked up their heads and strained to hear. The calls came again, closer this time.

"It's your brother," said the girl.

"What does he say?" asked Kasia.

They listened again.

"He's calling for dinner!"

The girl stepping in the stream caught sight of the other two getting up and threw down her pole at the base of a tree—a tree broken at its base and leaning into the water as if the stream were slowly pulling it along and re-shaping it over many decades. She ran splashing up to the shore and gathered up the two small fish she had caught from the muddy bank and rinsed them quickly in the water before wrapping them in the end of her dress that had been tied high around her waist. Then, without speaking, the three girls started running up the path that had been worn to the earth, the long blonde hair of Kasia flowing behind her in the wind.

At a place where the paths crossed among the sectioned fields, one of the girls—the one with the book—turned off and waved without a word and was lost among the grain. The other two girls continued on their way.

"Kasia!" called the boy again just as the two girls came up to him.

"I'm here!" she said, and without stopping they continued to run toward home, the boy trailing behind them, unable to keep up from the girls' long legs.

"What do you have there?" asked the mother when the two girls ran into the house through the crowd of chickens. The boy followed them and paused for a moment to throw a handful of pebbles at the birds.

"Fish!" said Anya with a gleaming smile, holding the fish out to show her and then putting them next to the sink. The older boy sitting at the table moved to get up and see, but the father stopped him with a raise of his hand. Then Anya walked over to the woman and took her infant brother from where he had been nursing in the woman's arms.

"Ma, can Anya stay for dinner?" asked Kasia.

"We do not have enough to eat already," said the woman, covering herself and fixing her dress. She looked sternly at her daughter. "Anya's brother has already taken enough from our mouths today." She looked at the young girl with short dark hair standing next to her. "This makes three children your mother has had me nurse. Even you, Anya, grew from my milk. It's a shame your own mother is so barren."

The girl was not listening to the woman but was playing with her brother, bouncing him in her arms.

"But we have fish now," pleaded Kasia.

"That's a baby fish," said the younger brother who was now standing at the door.

Kasia did not look at him or acknowledge the remark.

"That's enough," said the mother. She nodded as she took them in her hands and motioned for the girls to sit as she took out a pan to cook them.

At dinner, Kasia and Anya shared the same plate and fork, as the family had no extras. The mother remained at the wood stove and cooked the fish in oil and served them after everyone had nearly finished and she was able to sit and eat. With the fish, there was more than enough to go around, and Kasia was glad for this.

After they had eaten and Anya had returned home with her brother, the two boys sat at the table with their father learning cards from an old deck in the remaining light of the evening. Kasia looked over at them jealously while she helped her mother wash dishes.

"Anya told me her uncle can get shoes in town for half the price." said Kasia.

"You know we cannot buy shoes." The mother's voice cut her off quickly.

"But they won't cost much. They're used. I can even use my old laces."

The mother said nothing. Kasia understood this to mean she should not continue.

"We have no money for shoes," the father said over his cards without looking up. "What's wrong with the shoes you have on?"

Kasia looked down at her bare feet against the rough wood floor and said nothing. The sole pair of shoes she owned she wore only when she went into town or to church. She was afraid to get them dirty at home.

"We will get you new shoes for your birthday," the woman whispered to her daughter. "I promised you that last year. I'm saving a little money."

The father heard this and set his cards on the table. He looked at them blankly. There was a long stare and everyone waited for him to say something.

"Come on, Papa," said the younger brother. "It's your turn."

"Teodor!" shouted the mother.

The boy was quiet and looked back down at the table. There was silence for a moment longer until the father spoke.

He opened his mouth to speak and then paused. "There is talk that the factory is closing," he said softly.

There was silence in the room. Everyone looked at their father. The only sound was a chicken pecking away at the door frame.

"What does that mean?" asked Kasia quietly to her mother.

"I don't know," said the woman. She looked at her husband who had stood up from the table.

"There is a meeting tomorrow to talk about it," he said. "Some of the men are getting together to talk about it."

There was only silence. Kasia reached up to the carved angel hanging on the string around her neck and quietly said something.

That night, after the children had gone to bed, the woman lay down next to her husband who was staring blankly at the ceiling. "What would we do without the factory?" she asked. "We don't make enough food to eat as it is."

There was only silence. She wasn't sure she understood what all this meant. Finally, several minutes later, the man spoke.

"My father did not eat today," he said. "He has not eaten since Sunday."

There was a long silence between them. The woman hesitated. She did not want to say the words.

"Your father stopped breathing this evening," she said finally. "I am sorry. I did not want to tell you."

After some time, the man seemed to nod with acceptance. He thought about his job, about the factory, about the other men of the village. He thought about his sons and about the harvest and about the shoes they wanted to buy for Kasia. His sons would grow strong and would always have work. There was always work somewhere, as long as you had strong arms and a strong back. But then there was Kasia. They had thought to send her to school one day if they could find the time and the money for books. Kasia could make something of herself beyond the life on the farm. There was hope in his daughter—something beyond his own struggle, beyond simply surviving each day, as his own father had done. But then there was the news of the factory. He already knew when his last day of work was. He knew that he should have told his family that the closing of the factory had already been decided. But he had not been able to speak the words.

The man sighed heavily and said nothing. With effort, he reached up and blew out the kerosene lamp and watched as darkness filled the small, dirty room.

UP IN BAILEY TOWN

Jack's a bully and we all know it. I've never seen him lift a hand to anyone, but he doesn't have to. He's just mean as hell. We guys, we all get on him here and there just joking, like we do all of us, but Jack we give a little extra room because he knows how to make it bad for you. Just stay out of his way, that's the best we can do. Nothing else to do about it.

Now the only problem between me and Jack is that I'm married to his sister. Julia's her name. I met this girl in the checkout line at the grocery store a few years back in grad school, and we started going out. Turned out a few weeks later it was Jack's sister. I didn't know he had one. Certainly didn't know it at the time, or I probably would have stayed clear. So when he finds out he comes to me and tells me I can't see her anymore; and that's all fine with me, but then his sister throws a fit and tells him she's in love with me. So then, after that, I'm stuck. I've got to be on my best behavior from then on, or Jack'll kill me. Well, a year or two goes by, and then without me putting too much thought into it Julia and I end up getting married. Julia's great; but, looking back, that was a mistake. Tough times for me, but I've managed to make the best of it so far.

So it's me and Jack and my friend Bill from work that come to Bimini on a fishing trip. We're after mahi and wahoo and maybe a marlin or sailfish if we can dig one up in the Stream. That was the first two days, and then yesterday we hit the flats for bonefish with Bonefish Freddy. We've got a few more days of fishing ahead of us, but today we only went out in the morning. Didn't catch much. Too much sun and not enough beer.

I'm driving the golf cart we've rented from the shack across from the Blue Water Marina, and Jack's sitting next to me. Bill's riding on the seat behind us facing backward. We've all had a few beers today and I'm hitting every bump in the road, just to make it interesting for Bill.

"Damn it, Eddie!" says Bill, "What you hittin' all those bumps for?"

"Oh, sorry," I say. "I wasn't aiming for them." But I let out a little laugh because, of course, I was.

Bill laughs, too. "Damn it, Eddie!" he says. "You pull this shit thirty or forty more times, and we're gonna have a problem."

Bill's always been a joker. That's why I like hanging out with him. Always keeps you laughing. I'd quit my job if it weren't for Bill being there, making the days bearable.

We continue on up the island, and I keep hitting all the bumps and swerving all over the one-lane concrete and shell road that we share with carts and small trucks going both ways. Dodging and swerving, just for fun. I'm not used to driving on the left. I aim for a good pothole and hit it at full speed so that I see Bill bounce a bit off his seat behind me. That one hurt me a bit, too.

"Damn!" cries Bill. But he's laughing just as hard as I am.

"All right, all right," says Jack sitting next to me. "That's enough of that." I see out of the corner of my eye he's not smiling.

Bill and I were just having a little fun, but Jack didn't see the fun of it. I immediately slow down to about three-quarters speed and avoid all the bumps and potholes. I get real sober real quick. I was just trying to have a little fun, that's all.

Well, it's only a few short minutes heading north on King's Highway, the only main road that runs the whole length of the island, and we're leaving Alice Town and pass a sign that says "Welcome to Bailey Town" in big letters. I don't see much of a change from where we were, but I just shrug my shoulders and keep on driving. Funny place.

"Let's stop for a beer," says Bill. We had set out with no objective, maybe to go as far up the island as we could, so with the sun and the heat and no wind that sounds like a pretty good idea to me. I pull the cart over to a little pink and yellow building that says "BAR" painted in blue on the side. Lots of buildings that look like that. The engine shuts off on its own when I stop. We all get out, and we all head straight in for a cold drink and some shade.

I'm walking behind Bill and see him shaking his hands and arms wildly for no reason.

"Why the hell are you shaking like that, Bill?" I ask him.

"Jeez," he says, "I haven't had anything to drink today. Need a drink fast." But it's not true—we each had four or five beers on the boat this morning before we rented the cart, maybe more. Maybe his tank's just running low.

We go inside, Jack leading the way. When we walk into the place, there are already three men sitting at the bar and another two at a small table under the TV bolted on the wall. One of the three at the bar owns the place, and he gets up when we walk in. It's clear that everyone there had been inside all day to avoid the heat, and they look from the TV over to us when the light from outside flashes through the doorway as we walk in. Then they all turn back to their beers and to the TV. Some Bahamian news channel is on. No one says anything, but that's the way it was before we'd come in. The sand on the rough wood floor feels good under my sandals and reminds me why I like coming on these trips. I've never been to Bimini before this, though, and it seems nice enough. Jack and I take two stools at the end of the bar, and Bill grabs a metal chair with bad upholstery and pulls it up near us. The bartender hands us handwritten paper menus even though he's sure we're just there for a beer.

"You guys gonna eat anything?" Jack asks me. He looks quickly over the menu and tosses it back on the bar. Same food you see everywhere—cracked conch, conch fritters, and conch salad. Can't go wrong with any one of them, really. But we're not there to eat anything. Just need a cold drink.

"Nah, you?" I say.

"Nope, just a drink. Beer."

"Yeah, I'll go the same way," says Bill.

We order three Kalik Golds, and the bartender pulls them out slowly from an ice chest, shakes the cold water off, and pops each of the caps off. Then he slides them over to us across the worn wood bar.

"Twelve dollars, please," the man says in a deep island accent and smiles so that his three or four good teeth show between the other blackened ones.

I reach in my pocket for some wet bills and put them on the bar. "I've got this one, Jack. You get the next one."

Jack reaches for his drink and then stops.

"Hmm," he says, half under his breath and half to the bartender. "Twelve dollars? Three beers for twelve dollars?"

I look over at the bartender, and he just stands there with his same smile. "Yes, sir," he says. "Twelve dollars."

"Must be inflation," I say and push the bills and a tip over to the bartender.

"Twelve dollars?" says Jack, a little louder this time.

The bartender reaches down for the bills, but Jack reaches out and snatches them away.

"We're not paying twelve dollars for three beers!" says Jack. "I've never been charged twelve dollars. Not on any of these islands. We're not paying that."

"It's all right, Jack," I say. "I'm paying. Let's just have a drink." The day had been hot on the water and we hadn't caught anything decent. Nothing except a few macks that we threw back because we didn't want to clean them. With burned necks and sweat rolling down, all we had wanted on the ride back was another cold drink.

"No, Eddie," says Jack. "We're not paying twelve bucks for drinks. They don't charge the locals twelve bucks. We're paying six like everyone else." Jack counts out six bills from the ones I had laid down on the bar and pushes them toward the bartender. He hands me the rest.

"Jack," I say, "it's all right. I'm paying. We'll have one drink here and then we'll go somewhere else." I reach over to hand the bartender the rest of the money. By now, the other men in the bar have turned away from the TV and are looking over at us, but no one has said anything.

"No!" says Jack. He grabs the money from my hand. "I'm tired of being charged more just because we're not from here. We're paying six. Two dollars a beer like the other place." He slaps the six bills in front of the bartender and picks up his bottle and takes half of it down at once. "Drink your drink, Eddie," he says to me.

He waits for me to drink, but I just stand there. Then he takes his bottle and finishes the rest.

"Have your drink, Eddie. Bill, drink up. Then we'll have another." He turns to the bartender. "Three more," he says, "for six dollars."

The bartender doesn't move. He just looks at me with confused eyes. The smile on his face is gone. I don't see his teeth anymore.

"It's all right, Jack," I say. "We'll just go somewhere else."

"No," says Jack, turning again to the bartender. "Three more beers."

The bartender again stands there without moving. Mostly just uncertain.

"It's fine," I say to him.

"No," says Jack. "I disagree. They only charged us two bucks a beer at the other bar."

"It's fine," I say again.

"No," says Jack again. "I disagree."

"Well, I disagree louder!" Bill chimes in. He's just trying to make a joke and stop the trouble. We both look at him. Neither of us thinks it's very funny. Bill goes back to sipping his beer.

"Look," says Jack. "I'm not paying four dollars a drink. I'm paying two."

The menu is still face-up on the bar. I glance at it quickly and point down to it. "Jack," I say, "the price listed for Kalik Golds is four dollars a bottle. Right there on the menu."

But he doesn't look down to where I'm pointing.

"We're not paying four dollars a bottle," he insists. "We're paying two."

But behind us I hear the two men at the table under the TV start to stand up. I hear their chairs move on the wooden floor.

"Let's just go, Jack," I say. "We'll just go back to the store and get some beers there. Much cheaper there."

Jack stands there rolling the base of his bottle between his fingers on the bar. I can feel the two men standing behind us. Not close, but they're there.

"It's all right," I say to the man behind the bar. "We're just gonna go." I take a few more wet bills from my pocket and put them on the bar to pay for our beers. Then I take a big gulp from my bottle and head toward the door. I reach back and grab Jack's arm. "I think we should go, Jack," I say. I pull him along and feel him moving with me. I guess he saw the guys get up, too. Jack's still grumbling, but I don't hear what he is saying. All the while, none of the men in the bar says anything. I'm actually surprised I can get Jack out of there. Bill's right behind us with his beer in his hand.

Outside, the sun is hard on our eyes, even with our sunglasses, and we walk on the hard-packed white sand back to the cart.

"They have no right," Jack is saying. "They have no right to make us pay, just because we're god damn tourists," he says. "I've been coming here for ten years and never paid that."

"You're right," I say. "But let's just go back to the hotel and get a drink. I need a good cold one. Maybe a few."

We get back in the cart and I drive as fast as I can back to the hotel, avoiding all the bumps along the way. Once back, just a few minutes later, we park and walk over the dirty white concrete that's hot under our feet toward the hotel, and I can feel the sweat coming up again and start to drip down my back. Up ahead of us is the sound of a speaker playing calypso music that sounds farther away than it really is. When we get back to the dock at the Big Game, we see the fishing boats coming in off the Stream. The day is too hot and stale, and the fishing is done. They've all given up, just like we did, but there are still a few flags flying of the fish they've caught out on the clear blue water. Mahi, a few wahoo, and one sailfish.

"God damn thieves," Jack is saying under his breath as we walk up the steps to the bar. "Thieves!"

I had already forgotten about it, except I know we can't go back into that bar the rest of the time we're here.

Some days with Jack are good days, and some days aren't so good.

At the bar, overlooking the water over the flats with the fishing boats in the channel coming in with the sun on them, you can see far off in the direction of Andros and Nassau. Up above, way far out, there are a few dark clouds building, and I see a flash of lightning crawl through the cloud without reaching down to touch the water. But this far off you can't hear any thunder, and it almost doesn't look real. Maybe it'll bring some cool air with it.

"How about a drink?" I ask Jack.

"Sure," he says. "Fine, fine. God damn four dollars a beer. God damn thieves."

Bill looks at me and smiles. He knows I'm stuck. It's Julia's brother, for God's sake. Nothing I can do about it, and he knows it. "I think I need a good strong one myself," he says. "Something with a good swig of rum in it."

I look back at him as the waitress comes up with the menus. "Yeah, Bill," I say. "Me, too."

A KEPT MAN

Lunch hour at the Lyons Club nearly over, I sense the hurried rustle of the morning papers, the clang of shiny silver stirring spoons against the thin-walled Club china, the hurried attempts at discussing some important matter of business that cannot wait until later. All this before the men in dark suits rush back to their glass offices with heavy wooden desks and messages waiting that require their urgent consideration. It is a tension that swells in the air, felt by all, though any visible evidence of its cause is noticeably absent. I smile to myself as I overhear the man behind me try to close the deal he has been trying to close for months. The man he is speaking with grumbles audibly in annoyed avoidance as he moves to stand. I've heard this all before. The carrying on of business, of course, within the sturdy oak walls of the Club, is looked down upon, and is expressly forbidden in the Club Rules posted in the hall; but, if your voice is kept low around the more established members, certain rules tend to go unenforced. It's the way things have always been.

A young man, a newer member of the Club that I have met once before, hurries past, brushing against my sleeve and the thick leather chair near a warm but otherwise unoccupied fireplace where I sit idly. I say idly because I've been sitting here without serious thought for some time now. The young man looks back quickly with an apologetic glance to which I nod forgiveness, then hurries on. I really don't mind, though; in fact, a grin creeps across my face as I've grown quite accustomed to the daily ritual of such hurried movement, privileged that I can observe it all casually while leaning back and sipping from my warm glass of Scotch. In a few moments, the rush of a hundred woolen men out the door to brace the gray winter cold begins, as cattle through the slaughterhouse gates, and only then is the Club empty enough for the few who remain to appreciate it fully. And then I have my peace, and I have my silence, with my warm amber drink to keep me company. Because I do not have an office to run to. I am not compelled to muscle through the plastering snow and the crowded streets to be somewhere I don't want to be, simply to perform trivial tasks in return for an earned existence. Because I am not bound by clocks, nor charts, nor other self-imposed shackles. Because...well...let's just say that I am a man of leisure.

The particulars of such a position never did give me much thought. From the beginning, I did not deliberate on it all too long. Like many things in my new position, I'm just taking it all as it comes. I decided early on not to ask too many questions. It was a conscious choice—a revolt against my own mind and my natural tendency to dwell exhaustively on every aspect of something new until I fully grasped its meaning. Instead, I decided to let my subconscious sort it all out while I brooded over more important matters, like watching the lines of liquid run down the inside of my heavy leaded glass after a sip, or following the smooth blue streams of smoke rise from the end of the cigarette I'll have later. Because this world is real and I can touch it and devour it, observe it and manipulate it, embrace it willfully. It is not something stale and distant that I might have read in a case file—law school is behind me now. This is my time to live.

I've heard of women in this same position, of course—women who are, well...taken care of. You can find them in books and movies, or hear of them from a friend of a friend. But with women it all seems so cheap when you consider the reality of why they're there. With men it's quite different. Complex. Refined. I had never even thought it was a position meant for men, but it all seems so natural now. When you try to define it, none of the labels seem to stick. More than anything they only cheapen it.

"Man of Leisure" is something I've grown quite comfortable with—it's something I can live with and respect. Yet, I have to laugh sometimes when my mind lands on what I really am. At twenty-seven, with an Ivy League education and the most vigilant Presbyterian upbringing behind me, I am an accessory—an ornament, a possession owned by someone else. And not just by anyone. I am the property of Ms. Beverly Westling.

Now, the name Westling can be heard around many circles in New York. To the unacquainted, the name might be passed over with a loose recognition but without much thought. To those who know, however, it is a name worthy of the weight it carries in gold, silver bullion, timber groves, cumulative preferred shares, unsubordinated bonds...I could go on. A name tied to ever-increasing fortunes, both monetary and otherwise, of pedigreed American lineage, with a few curious twists along the way.

There is a long list of Westlings that can be recalled in the history of New York. There was Charles Arnold Westling, the financier, who founded the line back in 1805 with the establishment of the Southern Manhattan Trust Company; though the name found its way to America, as the family claims, in the summer of 1664 as part of a merchant enterprise to the Virginia Colony originating from Portsmouth. Real old stock, you might say. There was Henry Westling, the judge and railroad man. Henry James Westling, his son, who by the time he was forty had ensured the immortality of the family name by owning land

and buildings on nearly every city block south of 42nd Street that might be worth owning. Henry James, with his gift of skillful acquisition and his habit of collecting wives, fanned the flames of the Westling name and sent embers far across society. And not just society in New York. There were Westlings from Boston to Savannah by the end of the Civil War. Over two hundred years, the Westling name has entrenched itself firmly in American aristocracy and has remained relatively untarnished by the scandals that habitually claw at American families of wealth.

Now there were certainly bad leaves on the tree, and even a bad branch now and again: a child born to a mistress, a secret marriage to someone of a less exceptional class; but these were all dealt with swiftly and quietly so that there was little more than a whisper to be drowned out. The Westling name had become something of American royalty by the twentieth century, on par with names like Roosevelt, Morgan, and Rockefeller. There was Charles Gregory Westling, now Senator of Massachusetts; Kimberly Westling, a pillar of philanthropy to every cause that was so deemed worthy; Frederick Westling, owner of the largest chain of department stores across the northeast; and Chester Westling, founder of the Westling Law Group of New York when he bought two highly established firms and rolled them into one. It was this last spring of the Westling name that had brought forth Ms. Beverly Westling, formerly Beverly Plunkett of Steuben, Maine, who had married into the family at just seventeen and had inherited the fortunes and business holdings of Chester when he died three years later at the age of fifty-two.

Certainly, questions were raised about Chester's premature end, and it was eventually found that he had died of a heart attack, as his robust physique and fondness for heavy drink might suggest. But the appetite in the media for scandal pinned the death on Beverly after she admitted to a friend that Charles had once beaten her and locked her in a closet. They were known to clash in public, and fabricated stories by unnamed acquaintances quickly arose and found their way into print. The newspapers just ate it all up. Charges were filed by the State of New York at the family's request, but they were quickly dismissed when two separate autopsies confirmed his clogged heart.

But the biggest question of all, and the reason the family filed charges in the face of their normally hushed approach, arose over his immense stakes in everything from furniture factories to diamond mines. The Westling family initially tried to keep Miss Plunkett, as they officially referred to her in court documents, away from reporters, and to retain control of what they might lose of Chester's holdings. They argued that she had lied about her age on the marriage certificate, which of course she had done, but the courts dismissed this assertion as grounds for annulment. They even tried to buy her out—there were procedures in place for just such things. But young Beverly held out; and, with the help of a young lawyer she'd found in the phonebook because Chester's firm refused to represent her, she was able to keep the Westling name, as well as Chester's stakes in all his various holdings. In the end, the case rested on the fact that Chester had never taken any step to make up a proper will.

All this I learned over time from the various conversations I had with those surrounding Ms. Westling—not from Ms. Westling herself, of course. It took a while to piece it all together and to differentiate fact from rumor, as rumors tend to swirl around such infamous socialites. As for Ms. Westling herself, I not only knew nothing in the beginning of this woman who had taken me on, seemingly without my knowledge or my consent, but I also made the decision in keeping with my new perspective not to try and dig too deep. It simply wasn't my intent.

This Ms. Westling is the woman who now holds me in her hand. She owns me, and I have resigned myself to this fact. Not only resigned myself, I have embraced this, and the whole of my existence now relies upon it.

And so I sit here in the lounge of the Club alone, glad to have a little silence to get lost in, the only other soul being a marble bust of the Club founder Jeremiah Lyons that sits across the room on a shelf facing me. I give the statue a nod and a raise of my now empty glass and return to my reading, having switched from an article comparing French and English imperialism in Africa to a book comprised of short stories by several authors I've never heard of. The randomness of the books I pick up from the walls of the Club surprises me every day, as if there were no conscious selection made of the texts except how their binding matched the carpet at my feet. I wonder if they were really meant to be read at all. The essay I had read bored me, but I take it all in just the same, like some bitter pill that must be swallowed to become more cultured. It's something I simply must do. In the book of short stories, the first one engages me, the second leaves me uneasy. I set it down and shake my glass to get at the last of the Scotch and then set the glass on the table next to a stack of books that has been following me around the Club all morning. The sun has moved behind a building outside the window, leaving sharp rays surrounding its form in the falling snow, so I reach over and pull the chain on the glass lamp, though it is really not that dark in the room. An attendant comes by in a minute and brings me another glass of Scotch. I quickly reach and try to sip a last drop from my glass before handing it away. Then I take a sip from the new one and wish I had ordered something mixed instead. But the attendant has vanished, and I am left alone with Mr. Lyons and with my books; and, in a moment, the drink resonates within me and I am warmed once again.

Becoming cultured, as I said, is something I have taken on with full sincerity. My mother had once enrolled me in etiquette classes and dancing lessons when I was young. She said they would prove their worth in time. I resisted entirely and looked to my father for salvation every time my tie was being tied and my hair was being straightened, but he only nodded quietly and turned back to his paper and left the matter to my mother. Those went on every week for six years before my grumbling finally wore her down. There is something to be said for her Presbyterian persistence. But the difference now is that I choose my own instruction. Scotch is the newest thing I have taken up. It's my newest hobby, you might say. I have taken on new things here and there along my path to becoming a bit more sophisticated. I'm not exactly sure what that means, of course, but I know that it involves an appreciation for many things—things that might take some getting used to. I've also taken up smoking and foreign films. Mostly Italian. Pasolini and Fellini and the like. Darker stuff. Smoking caught on pretty quickly—I've learned to always have a cigarette at least handy. And reading. Reading has emerged as the greatest source of my learning. I had always looked on it as if it were a chore, as most people do; something that was required of you because someone with authority told you to do it and because you were going to be tested on it. I never imagined it as anything else. But here in the Club, where I found myself alone more and more, as everyone else had an external occupation, my nescient boredom turned to the walls and to the books contained within. It first started with the rack of newspapers near the bar because I needed something to make me look occupied while I sat alone with my drink in the early afternoon. After a few weeks I turned to each of the walls around me, choking down a few volumes at first, despite the fear of facing my own ignorance, and then becoming fully engulfed in the pages that unfolded before me. Every idea ever captured on paper, it seemed, was now accessible to me. Classic literature, which I had always feared I would be unable to grasp, turned out as entertaining as the penny pulp and comics I had bought as a kid. It was all there: lust, bar fights, murder, hedonism. It was all there to be consumed. But finishing a book and returning it to its shelf, this above all else, gave me the satisfaction I sought on my path of self-education, as if I now owned that which it contained. After a few months, when the books in the Club weren't enough, I started visiting small bookstores on the way back to my apartment, buying used novels for a quarter apiece—anything to satisfy my newfound appetite. The stacks of books in my apartment grew until I had to have another bookshelf installed to contain them.

And the list of new things I would try grew daily. New drinks, new authors, new museums, new paths to walk to new parks. The City was the place to take in culture, if ever there were such a place, and I thrived on the theory that I needed to undertake all of it. Good or bad, I live by consuming the world around me. When had I ever had an opportunity such as this, to try everything new without consequence? Being owned by someone is not a curse, it is a gift! I had known little of New York, having grown up far upstate and visiting it only once when I was too young to understand what I saw. It was a new thing to me now—something else to be consumed and explored. The mad rush of people. The streets lined with cars. The center of fashion and finance and culture. The world re-volves around this place. But it had only been an idea in my mind, until now. Now this is my world, and yet there is so much in it that is unknown to me.

The Club is on 44th between Fifth Avenue and Grand Central. My apartment is in a 'quiet' neighborhood in Midtown East. My walks to the museums and theaters I do not mind, even in the heavy snow and biting cold of winter. I could have the car take me, but I enjoy the walks. In the fall it wasn't so bad. More of the City to explore. More people to see. More of everything to take in. It is still all new to me, even after these few months; and for the first time in my life I am conscious of it all. Everyone around me is in a rush to get somewhere, to do something, to become someone else. But me, I have the luxury of time before me, and the luxury of money beneath me. It is a lifestyle I am settling into quite nicely. Mornings at a new café, always trying something from the menu I've never had; walks along a quiet residential street or through the crowds of Times Square; early lunch at the Club where I talk with friends before watching them head back off to work so that I am left with the book I had picked up a few days before. In the afternoons I might catch the subway for an hour and study the people until I get bored with this and get off at a random stop. I'd like to see every neigh-borhood in Manhattan, if only for a moment, though my approach has been less than systematic. Some days I wake up early, some days I sleep late. Very rarely do I find myself bored. But the one thing I never do is take any of this for granted. In my admittedly short life to this point I have labored and I have worked hard, and so I feel in a way that I deserve all this, as if it were all destined for me. Yet, I know that it is conceivably by chance that I have been afforded this life of privilege—Ms. Westling simply happened to see me in the elevator on the way to her law firm where I worked one morning, and took an interest in me. And so I cannot disparage my fate or anything that comes with it.

But being a man in my position is not all liberty and pleasure. There are responsibilities. There are duties to be performed. And, of course, there is the act itself. Even the bird in the golden cage must be called upon to sing from time to time. Every whim, every impulse, every moment I am to be on call, just in the case that I am needed. In the beginning, this kept me on edge, and I stared at my phone for hours waiting for a call. But after a few weeks, I noticed a regular pattern, and I was usually called upon for an evening just two or three times a week with ample warning of an hour or two, if not a day. Her people are always very good about that. If I cannot be reached on my phone for some reason, they know they can usually find me at my apartment or here at the Club. There are fantastic dinner parties, balls, and charity banquets. Not every night, but often enough to keep me socially interested. Though just more than twice my age, Ms. Westling not only has a vigorous appetite for physical pleasure, but also for social appearances. But she has never called on me unexpectedly or shown up in her town car at my apartment unannounced; yet it is understood that I do make myself available to her on any occasion she wishes. I have not dared to find out what might happen if I did not present myself as expected. There is no reason to test this, of course. I decided at the beginning that I would play by the rules set out for me without question, because the bulk of my time is my own. Never once have I rebelled against my situation. Nor will I. There is simply nothing to be gained from it.

I look down at my glass and see that it is nearly empty, having sufficiently warmed me against the inevitable cold that I must brave outside. That was several glasses ago now, I think; I've lost count. The attendant has come many times without me noticing and replaced my glass. I set down my book and realize that after finishing all but the last short story I have been staring at the page without reading for half an hour now, distracted instead by the ticking of the clock in the empty Club room. There are certainly others here among the many chambers of this place, but they are not within view—others, like me, and for whatever reason, who can afford the avoidance of other responsibilities for the pursuit of leisure, the most noble of all pursuits.

I check my watch and see that it is nearly five o'clock. A pair I recognize from lunch wanders back into the Club for an afternoon drink. An unnecessary sense of urgency descends upon me and I close my book and set it among the things on the table. Just then the attendant arrives with another glass.

"I'm sorry," I say with a wave of my hand. "I have to run."

The waiter, of course, on returning to the kitchen, enjoys the glass of Scotch on me, as it has already been charged to my account. I would have done the same. Besides, my quite substantial allowance permits me never to think of money. It's all taken care of.

I bundle myself in wool at the door and hurry needlessly out to the town car that is waiting for me. The driver takes me down the frozen street, up the few blocks to 53rd, and east to my apartment. Inside, a long hot shower and all the ceremonies that precede and follow it ensure that I look, smell, and feel the way that Ms. Westling expects me to. When I finish and look at myself in the mirror, I fix my cufflinks and straighten the lapel of my dinner jacket. I look at my watch and know that another car will arrive for me in exactly thirty-five minutes. I'm glad I left the Club when I did—just enough time for a taste of Scotch, a cigarette, and to finish the last story from the book I had swiped from the Club. But, as I read, I wait anxiously for the ring of the driver at the door. A lady should never be kept waiting—especially the one to whom you owe your well-appointed existence.

INTERMISSION

I t was a four act play, and it was a long one. They had already been in their seats for over an hour. Plus, it was opening night, so there were still a few kinks to be worked out yet. It all seemed to drag on a bit, thought Dennis. When he had agreed to come to the play, he hadn't known he was buying tickets for the opening night. But he was already here, he thought, and he might as well do his best and try to enjoy it.

Finally, the big red curtain came to a close, the lights came up, and the music started for the intermission. Dennis came back to reality and looked timidly over at the girl next to him without speaking. They sat and waited until the people to their right had cleared the row, then they stood up.

"Want to get a drink?" he asked her.

"Sure," she said.

The girl's name was Hattie. Dennis wondered if that were short for Heather or something. Or maybe her last name. This date had been a set-up, and he found that a bit amusing because this girl was pretty enough. Weren't all blind dates supposed to be plump girls with great personalities? Well, by her looks, maybe she were selfish or unbelievably dull or something.

He was ahead of her as they made their way through the crowd. Hundreds of people were darting for the exits all at once. Then he felt a soft, cool hand on his. He looked back at the girl and smiled and grasped her hand as he led her through the dense crowd.

In the lobby of the theater, at the bar, it was immensely crowded as well. There were long lines leading towards the restrooms and to the bar where there were only three servers pouring glasses of wine and popping the tops off beers. The longest line was for the women's restroom, and the next longest was all the men at the bar. It was a horrible play—they would all need drinks to get them through it.

"Pretty crowded!" shouted Dennis as he made his way toward the bar. "I wonder if we'll even get up there."

Hattie stood back a step while he fought his way forward. It was pretty fruitless. They were all pushing against one another to get nowhere.

"Hey!" she called out to him after a minute or two. He looked back and saw her waving to him. "Come on!"

Confused, Dennis left his place in line and went back to her. Maybe she didn't want a drink, he thought.

"I know where we should go," she said. "Follow me."

She led him through the crowd, hand-in-hand so that they wouldn't get separated, and out the heavy ornamented metal doors onto the sidewalk. The street was completely empty now except for a few couples passing by, and it was a nice relief from the crowded lobby inside. The girl pulled him down off the sidewalk, away from the theater, and across Geary Street to the buildings beyond.

"Let's get a drink in here," she said as she motioned to the lit-up bar ahead of them. "This place has good drinks."

As they were crossing the street, Dennis was reflecting on the girl that was leading him. Bringing someone he'd never met before to a play might not have been the best idea. All they could do was just sit there silently next to each other and stare blankly ahead. He couldn't talk with her or learn anything about her. He couldn't talk about himself. He certainly didn't know anything about her so far, as they had both been running late and had only met at the ticket booth just as the play was about to start. But her face was quite pretty, he thought, if you didn't mind the heavy makeup. She did have an interesting style about her, though. She wore a dark blue dress that was so dark it looked black, and she had on metallic silver lipstick and a little ring in her lip. He had never dated a girl with a lip ring before. But she was actually very pretty. Her hair was dyed jet black and cut short, and her makeup was very heavy around her eyes. She looked a bit freakish to him, but she did it in such a way that it was rather pleasant. She was tall, too. And thin. Your eyes were drawn to her. And her voice was smoky and smooth. All of the other girls he had been out with since arriving in San Francisco three months ago had been so plain and boring. But there was definitely something different about this girl. She projected a certain confidence that left him troubled, slightly afraid of her.

Inside the bar, it was warm and cozy, and Dennis hadn't noticed that it had been cold outside, but now he felt it. He didn't see anyone in there except the man behind the bar looking at a folded newspaper. They went up to the bar to order a drink.

"What would you like?" he asked her.

"Something with gin," she said. "I like gin."

He liked gin, too, he thought. Most girls didn't, that he had known. They all stuck to vodka.

The bartender, a heavy man with a gray ponytail, came up to take their order.

"I'll have an in-and-out Hendrick's martini, please," she said. "Three olives, if that's all right."

The bartender nodded.

Pretty nice choice, Dennis thought to himself. He might get the same, but he didn't want to copy her and seem dull.

"Um," he said, "I'll have a Negroni. Ahh...Hendrick's as well." It was another good gin drink he liked. Sometimes he wasn't in the mood for the Campari, but it would be all right for tonight.

The girl looked over at him. "Nice," she said. "I like those, too. A bit bitter, but I like them."

They waited there a minute in silence as the bartender pulled the bottles and glasses to make their drinks. Dennis wasn't sure if he should lean so that his arm touched hers, or if he should ask her something about herself, or what. So he just stood there leaning against the bar without a word, trying to seem confident and casual.

"I like your lipstick," came a woman's voice from down the bar.

Dennis looked up and saw that there was an older couple at the bar in the corner. He hadn't seen them there when they had walked in. There was no one else in there besides them. The man was in a suit that was slightly too big for him, and the woman wore a nice lime-green dress and pearls around her neck and in her ears. They looked stylish, but from a few decades ago.

"Oh," Hattie blushed. "Thank you, ma'am."

"I like that color," the woman said. "It's very bold. I like it." Her husband nodded hello to them but focused more on the drink in front of him than on the conversation.

"Thank you," said Hattie. "It's my favorite color."

Dennis smiled at her.

"And I like your ring," the woman continued. "Does is hurt in your lip like that?"

The girl laughed a little. She had heard the question so many times. "No," she said. "It hurt when I got it, of course, but it was only a little bit. It doesn't hurt now. But thank you for the compliment."

The Negroni and the martini came, and Dennis and Hattie each raised their glasses with a clink and took a big sip. Then they raised their glasses over to the woman down the way, and they all had a sip. Dennis looked at his watch.

"How long until the play starts back up?" he asked her.

"I don't know," she said.

The woman spoke up. "It's about fifteen minutes," she said. "Curtain to curtain. This one might be twenty since it's the first night. Just long enough to stand in line and not reach the bathroom. That's why we always come over here. We can get a drink right away, and Fred can go pee." The man seemed to squirm in his seat, then he took another sip of his drink. They were drinking their drinks very slowly, enjoying them. "Do you like the play?" the woman asked them.

"Yeah," said Dennis. He lied. "It's pretty interesting so far."

"Oh," said the woman, "I think it's pretty boring. No storyline. Bad set. Bad acting."

"Yeah," said the girl. "I don't like it either."

Dennis wished he'd said that he didn't like it.

"You two married?" the woman asked.

Dennis and Hattie looked at each other awkwardly for a moment.

"Well…," started Dennis.

"Yes!" said Hattie. "Tonight's our first anniversary. We're out celebrating."

Dennis looked over at her, but Hattie returned with a smile and a wink that told him just to go with it. He smiled back.

"Oh!" said the woman. "Congratulations! You're very cute together."

"Thank you," they both said at the same time.

"We've been married for forty-three years," said the woman. "Can you believe that? Forty-three years!"

"No," said Hattie. "You look so young."

The woman smiled. "Thanks, dear. That's very nice of you. What brings you to this horrible play, of all the other places you could be celebrating tonight?"

"Well," said Dennis, "one of my friends is one of the minor actors. You wouldn't recognize him. He's the one that plays Fitch. Over on the right of the stage. He's only got a few speaking lines. Other than that he just comes and goes and stands there with his arms folded."

"Oh," said the girl next to him softly so that only he could hear. "I know Peter. He mentioned to me that he was going to be in this play. That's why I wanted to see it."

Interesting, thought Dennis. Peter was one of the better friends he had made since he'd moved here, but he had never mentioned this girl before. Maybe their circles of friends were closer than he thought. But this was the first time he had ever met her. Maybe Peter had wanted to keep her for himself. He could see why.

"Well," said Dennis, looking at his watch, "we should get back. We don't want to be locked out."

"Yeah," said Hattie. "Peter would be pretty upset if we missed the second half. He said most of his lines are in the second half."

Dennis reached out to pay the bill, but Hattie had already pulled cash out.

"I'll get this one," she said. "You can get another one later on."

"All right," he smiled. "Sounds good to me."

She paid the bill, and they finished the rest of their drinks quickly, laughing as they gulped them down. Dennis knew that the drink would hit him once he sat down and would help get them through the third act.

"Are you to heading back in as well?" Hattie asked the woman.

The man next to her grumbled and took another sip from his glass.

"Nah," the woman laughed, "I think we'll enjoy our drinks and then get on back home. It's enough effort for me to get him all dressed up and get him out the door. But keeping him out late is absolutely impossible. Still, it's nice to get out now and then. He promises me a night out once a month, and tonight it's the thirty-first. So he couldn't get out of this one!"

"Well," Hattie said with a giggle, "you can come with us if you want. We have an empty seat right next to us. We're right in the middle. You can come and join us for the rest of the evening if you want."

"Oh," said the woman, "that's very sweet of you two. But I think I'll get Fred back home and get him to bed. He doesn't like to stay up late."

The man grumbled again.

"Ok," said Dennis. "You enjoy the rest of your evening."

They moved to leave. But then Hattie stopped and turned to the woman.

"You know, ma'am, you look very pretty tonight," she said. "And I think you're very nice. You look so wonderful in your green dress and pearls, and I like your hair the way it's curled up like that. It's very cute. You're a very pretty woman."

"Well!" said the woman. "Thank you, dear! You make me blush. That's very sweet of you." She turned to her husband. "See, Fred, that's what a compliment sounds like!"

The man only shook his head and grumbled again.

"You two have a wonderful night then!" said the woman.

"Thank you," said Hattie. "Good night to you, too."

Dennis smiled. She was very pleasant, this girl. She made him smile. He reached and took down the last few drops of melted ice from his glass, just to get the last of the taste of the drink. Then he took her hand.

"Goodbye!" Hattie said to the woman.

She nodded back with a smile.

"Goodbye!" said Dennis with a wave.

Outside the bar they felt the coolness of the evening hit them again.

"That was nice," said the girl. "She was fun."

"Yeah," said Dennis. "I liked her." He squeezed the girl's hand and pulled her closer to him. They stepped down from the sidewalk and into the street, and as they did so she squeezed his hand back. They saw the theater doors closing ahead of them, and they quickened their step to get across. They would have to hurry to get back for the second half of the play.

OUT ON CROOKED CAY

"She's a feisty one, Andy," Dan said. Andy was mad that he'd said it. He didn't need to say it. "A real feisty one," Dan went on. "She's gonna make this trip fun."

They both took a sip from their glasses, and there was only silence afterwards.

The girl had arrived on the small island only a few minutes earlier on the little ferry boat from George's Cay in a whirlwind of suitcases and screaming complaints. It was a side of her Andy had never seen before, but then again he had only known her for two weeks. He was already regretting the decision to invite her along.

George's Cay was the closest island with an airstrip where the plane could land; and since she didn't want to come the day before with everyone else in Dan's plane, she had had to come on her own from Miami by way of Nassau. Her arrival set them all on edge the moment she stepped off the boat.

Andy didn't want to hear it from Dan. He knew it was coming, and he didn't want to hear any of it. After a few more minutes of silence between them he got up and went to see that Paula was getting settled.

"All I wanted was a little shade. And the man on the boat yelled at me," Paula began as soon as Andy opened the door, as if he'd been there all along. "He didn't have to talk to me that way." She was going between an open suitcase and the mirror, fixing her makeup. The three matching suitcases sat at the foot of the bed, all opened. There were other matching bags strewn about. It was more than enough for the three-day trip. "I don't know why people have to be so rude to me. I'm not rude to them."

Andy didn't say anything. He didn't have anything to say. Nor would it have helped anything.

"The flight was awful. The wait at the airport was awful. The wait to get my luggage was awful. They didn't even have a bathroom on the plane! Can you believe that? And there were fumes from the engine coming in through the window. I couldn't breathe! The flight made me sick." She wiped her face with a cloth and dug in a bag for something to put on her eyes. Her face never left the mirror the whole time. She went on. "There was a little black boy in front of me on the plane. He kept fiddling with the air vent or whatever, and he was letting the air in, and it was making me sicker and sicker. I slapped his hand away, but he just laughed and kept on doing it!"

Andy had barely shut the door when he had come in when he decided he didn't want to be there. He moved away and opened the door quietly behind her and slipped out without her knowing. Through the door he heard her start up again, but he wouldn't be there to listen to it.

"She'll be all right," Andy said when he got back out to Dan who was sitting back with his legs crossed and holding up another fresh drink for him. "Thanks. She'll be all right once she gets settled and she gets a few drinks in her."

But things didn't get better, and when they all sat down to dinner that Dan's wife Jessie had made from the snapper that Dan and Andy had caught under the dock, things only got worse.

"This fish is dry," said Paula flatly, poking at it with her fork.

They all sat there unable to speak while she went on. Andy thought the snapper was fantastic. Not only was it caught fresh not more than a few hours before, but Jessie had cooked it the only way he liked it—with butter, lime, and several heavy splashes of dark rum. He eagerly took the rest from Paula's plate to show Jessie he liked it, and Paula had more of the green beans and potatoes. She liked the potatoes and mentioned this several times. Andy laughed to himself because he knew that those had come out of a can. He felt bad for Jessie, and he would apologize to her later.

After dinner, Paula went to her room because the mosquitoes were getting her. But Andy and Jessie and Dan stayed out on the dock. They all drank heavily and didn't mention Paula. They all tried to forget about her and to just enjoy themselves.

"Tomorrow will be good fishing," said Dan. They all agreed. "The mahi are pretty thick on the weed lines, and Tommy back on George's Cay said they've been getting a sail or two each day. Small, but they're there. Should be a good trip."

Andy knew it was his fault for bringing Paula along. You don't take a girl on a fishing trip that hasn't proven she can do it, especially on a trip like this. He was embarrassed, and Dan knew it. If tomorrow were slow, they could troll all day and never get a hit. For Andy and Jessie and Dan, they would still love it even if there were no fish. They could catch up together and get drunk on rum and beer and the fumes from the diesel engines mixed with the salt spray. But not Paula. She would get bored and would probably get sick anyway. She'd spend half the day hanging over the side chumming the water. They weren't looking forward to the trip anymore.

The three of them stayed up late drinking and laughing until it was time to go to bed. They had to get up early to prepare the bait, make some sandwiches, and throw the coolers and ice together. Andy went in and found Paula asleep and did his best not to wake her. He didn't even want to wake her up for sex. Paula grumbled and rolled over, but then she went back to sleep. She had one of those pink sleep masks covering her eyes. Andy lay there in the bed awake, staring at the ceiling and hearing the waves outside. The drinks made everything swirl a bit. He was hot and wanted to go back outside in the breeze and sit looking at the stars, but he didn't want to get up and wake up Paula and get her going again. She would be mad at him for leaving her alone in the room so long. So he did his best to fall asleep.

In the morning, Dan woke Andy up early, before the sun was up, and they got the baits ready and filled all the coolers with ice and beer and ice for the fish, and then they sat down and talked until the sun came up.

"Feelin' it?" asked Dan.

"Yeah, I'm feelin' it."

"It's all right," said Dan. "You'll feel better once we're underway. A drink or two and your head will feel better."

Watching the sun come up was always a good feeling, and Andy hadn't seen a sunrise in a year or two. He was sad for that, but he was happy that he could watch it with Dan here on their island.

"Why don't you go get Paula and we'll head out?" Dan said. He hadn't wanted to say it. Jessie was already on the boat cutting bread and cheese for the sandwiches.

Andy went up to the house and knocked on the door and went in by Paula. She was still asleep, and he knew it was a bad idea to wake her. He hesitated for a minute. Whatever he decided next would determine which way the day went. But the fact that he was even thinking of it decided it for him. He slipped back out of the room as quietly as he could.

"Where's Paula?" asked Dan as Andy hopped aboard.

"Oh, she decided not to come. She was still feeling sick from the flight and wanted to sleep in." He was lying, but he knew it was best for all of them. Dan and Jessie would surely not be upset.

The day on the water was the best day Andy and Dan had fished in as long as they could remember. Each of them—Andy, Jessie, and Dan—each hooked and landed more than seven or eight small mahi apiece, Dan got a king mackerel, Jessie got a sail on and lost it on its fifth jump, and Andy got a decent wahoo in the boat. Jessie looked good in her orange bikini, and Dan didn't mind that Andy looked at her. He liked showing her off. They were all smiling and sunburned and drunk on beer and rum when the boat pulled back into the dock with two coolers full of fish. Paula heard them coming and came out of the house down to the dock. It was already getting dark.

"Where the hell have you been?!" she screamed. The mood on the boat plummeted as they tied up. Andy jumped off and walked her back into the house as he tried to explain. He didn't want Jessie and Dan to see.

Dinner that night was both a happy and uncomfortable feast. They grilled up the mahi with lime and a touch of brown sugar. Paula didn't eat any. She hardly ate anything and she hardly spoke. But Dan, Andy, and Jessie talked madly about the day. That night, Paula went to bed early and Andy didn't mind, and he stayed up drinking again with Dan and Jessie. It was the best day and the best night they'd had together in years.

"Why don't we do this more often?" asked Andy.

Dan laughed. "Because you have a stupid job and never get out here." It was true. Dan had been inviting him out for two years. The plane, the boat, and the house were always available for him.

"I'll make sure to get away more often then," said Andy. "This was worth it. I'm never going back to work again!"

"You're always welcome here, Andy," said Jessie. "It gets a little lonely out here sometimes because we're out here so often and there's no one close by. We're glad to have you."

As the night went on, no one talked about Paula. There was nothing to do about it anyway. Andy got up once and invited her out for a drink, just to be nice, but she stayed in the room and said she didn't want to be out by the mosquitoes.

Toward midnight, with more than a few drinks in each of them, Andy and Dan got the notion to go fishing along the shore as the tide ran out. It was close to a half moon with lots of light, and the tide would be strong going out. Dan had done it many times and had hooked up on nearly every cast with live shrimp each time he did it. They didn't have any live shrimp, but they could cut up some pinfish for bait and throw them out with the current. All they had to do was take the little aluminum boat Dan had tied up to the dock. Jessie was tired and wanted to get to bed and let the boys have their fun, so she stayed in.

"Don't come back smelling all fishy!" she shouted to Dan as she went up to the house. "I want some good lovin' when you get back."

"Yes, ma'am!" called Dan.

"You've got a good one there," Andy said to Dan.

"Yeah, she's great. She puts up with me. What more could I ask for? Hey," said Dan, "why don't you see if Paula wants to come with us?"

They both laughed, and then Andy thought it might not be a bad idea. Of course she wouldn't go. It was late and she was already upset at him. But he would get a few points for asking. And then she'd know he'd be out late.

He opened the door to their room quietly, and she rolled over half asleep.

"Hi, Paula," he said timidly. "Dan and I are going fishing in the little boat around the shore. Do you want to come with us?"

She took off her mask and pondered this for a moment. "Sure, I'll go," she said and started to get up.

Andy froze. He hadn't expected her to say yes.

"It's gonna be pretty rough and there're lots of mosquitoes out," said Andy, trying to convince her to stay. He was sorry he'd asked.

"I'll bring a long sleeve shirt and some spray," she said. Andy was silent. And in five minutes she was ready to go.

"Paula's coming with us," called Andy as Dan was getting into the boat with the poles and bait. "Do you have another life jacket?"

Dan, of course, was stunned that she was coming, and he laughed as he got another rod and life jacket. The three of them headed out not far around the sand spit to where they could get out of the boat and tie it up and walk along the shore with their poles. Paula was forcing a smile the whole time in the light of the moon.

Andy helped Paula with the bait and got her to throw the bait out, then he went to his own gear, and Dan already had one on. They weren't going to keep any of the fish, so they threw them back when they caught them. In a few minutes, Andy and Dan each had three small snook or snapper. Nothing big, but at least they put up a fight. Paula, still holding her pole against the current, hadn't gotten a bite.

"Let me reel it in for you," he said.

"I'll do it!" she said. She reeled the line in and there was no bait and only a hook.

"I'll get you a new bait." Andy went and baited the hook again and threw it out for her. A few minutes later, Andy and Dan each had another pair of fish, and Paula still had none. She reeled in her line again and there was only the bare hook.

"I'm going to go sit in the boat," she said.

"Try one more bait," said Andy.

"No, it's all right," said Paula, still forcing a smile. "I'll just go and sit down for a bit."

Andy went back to his rod and genuinely felt sorry she hadn't caught anything. Paula went back to the boat that was pulled up to the shore with the anchor pulled up tight in the sand, just in case the tide knocked the boat loose.

All of a sudden, there was a loud noise and bumping in the boat and a scream. Andy ran over to the boat that stood out in the moonlight.

"You all right?" Andy asked.

"I'm fine," Paula said with a whimper. He saw that she was half laughing and half crying.

"You sure?"

"I'm fine!" she said again.

Andy watched her for a minute as she got herself up onto a bench and sat there with her head in her hands.

"Are you hurt?"

"No, I'm fine!" she said again. "Just go back to fishing."

Now Andy really felt bad for her, but there was nothing he could do for her.

"She all right?" asked Dan when he had made his way back. He hadn't seen what had happened, but he'd heard all the noise.

"I'm sure she's fine," said Andy. "We'll just catch a few more and then head back. This is good fishing tonight. All day, really. This is great."

When Andy and Dan made their way back to the boat, Paula was sitting there with her cell phone screen lighting up her face.

"I can't get any reception," she said seriously.

Andy rolled his eyes.

"You won't get any here," said Dan. "We're way too far from any towers out here."

But Paula sat there shaking her cell phone, pressing the buttons, wondering why it didn't work.

They piled the gear in, and then Andy threw in the anchor from the sand and shoved them off, and they all rode back together. It was three in the morning when they got back, and they all went straight to sleep.

Before the sun came up, Andy rolled over in bed and felt that Paula was not there. He called out softly and then looked all around the dark room and didn't see her anywhere. He got up and quietly looked around the house and went out to the dock, but he didn't see her. He didn't want to wake up Dan, but he was afraid something had happened.

"I'm sure she just went for a walk," said Dan. But then he got up and they both looked around the house and out by the dock and down the sand road that led to the other side of the island, but they didn't see her anywhere. At the dock, Dan saw that the little aluminum boat was gone.

"She's taken the jon boat," he said. Without a word they both jumped onto the bigger boat and Dan fired up the engines while Andy untied the dock lines.

The sun was just breaking the water, bringing morning with it, when they came out of the channel. They scanned out over the horizon from the high bridge of the boat. It wasn't three minutes before they saw the jon boat far out, but she wasn't running. The boat was just sitting there. They came up to her fast and slowed right next to her. Paula was sitting to one side with one paddle hanging out of the boat.

"Where the hell are you going, Paula?" Andy called with a laugh.

"I'm going home," Paula grumbled. "I want to go home!"

Dan pulled the boat up next to her, and Andy jumped in. "Why are you paddling then?" he asked.

Paula kept paddling even though he was now in the boat with her. "Because I couldn't get the motor started. I didn't have the key."

Andy reached back and pulled the cord on the motor, and it started on the first pull.

Paula stopped paddling. She let the oar go in the water and threw her face into her hands and started crying loudly. Andy reached over the side and grabbed the oar and threw it in the boat. "Where's the other oar?" he asked.

"I dropped it in the water."

"Why'd you do that?"

"I didn't do it on purpose! I was trying to row. I just want to go home."

Andy laughed to himself as Dan stood looking down at them confused. She hadn't gone anywhere except where the current had taken her.

"I'll take her back in this," Andy said, and he waved to Dan as Dan went back up to the bridge and threw the engines into gear and headed back home. Andy followed in his wake in the little jon boat. He said nothing to Paula who was just sitting there crying. She hadn't even put her suitcases in the boat with her.

After they got back, and after Jessie and Andy and Dan had breakfast, Dan agreed to take Paula back to George's Cay where she could get on that day's flight back to Nassau, and then back to Miami. It was agreed that it was better for Andy not to see her off. He knew she didn't want to see him anyway. Andy and Dan silently loaded her suitcases onto the boat, and Andy and Jessie waved as they left. Dan waved back, but Paula did not. She just stared straight ahead.

"Nice girl!" Jessie joked as they watched the boat drive away.

"Thanks," said Andy.

"Well," said Jessie, "at least she was better than the last one. What was her name? Melanie?"

Andy laughed. "Yeah, Melanie."

The sad thing was, she was right.

THE RAINY SEASON

"You know," said Simon, looking closely into the polished steel of the window frame, "I have no idea how I got this scar."

"Hmm?" said Claire. She did not look up from her magazine.

Simon stared at himself, moving his fingers about his face in the reflection for a good several minutes before he answered. He had not brought anything to read, or anything to occupy himself, so his own reflection was the only thing to keep him busy. "Right here," he said, pointing at his eyebrow. "I think I've always had it. But I think that I do remember not having it. It's not in pictures from when I was really young. Hey...you're not looking!"

Claire sighed and looked up at him with a roll of her eyes.

"Right here," he said, "through my eyebrow. It's not that noticeable, of course. It's just there. I have no idea where it's from."

She leaned toward him, disinterestedly, but didn't see anything. "Never noticed," she said and looked back down at the page.

"Well," said Simon, "I guess I only notice it sometimes. I must have gotten in a fight when I was a kid or something. Or maybe I fell. I just don't remember."

The train wasn't far outside of Sanremo on the Italian coast when it came to a stop between stations. They were on their way to Ventimiglia where they would have to change to a French train heading toward Monaco. The train had left Imperia a few minutes before, made a few stops in towns that Simon did not know, and was now stopped on the tracks.

"We're stopping," said Simon, only after they had stopped moving. He noticed there were not any station signs out the window.

Claire looked up from her magazine. "I knew we should've taken the car," she said. "I wanted to take the car."

"Well," said Simon, "I like the train. I guess it is a few minutes longer with the change. I just hate worrying about parking and..."

"No one takes the train anymore," she said under her breath without looking up.

He paid no attention. "I like the train. I just can't face backward, that's all. I don't know how you can face backward like that. It makes me feel sick."

"I'm fine," she said. "It doesn't bother me."

"Well, I can't face backward. I get sick. I have to face toward the front."

It was three or four minutes before anything happened. Claire went back to her magazine, and Simon went back to studying his face in the dull reflection. Finally, there was a click from the speakers in the ceiling, and the conductor came on in a scratchy voice.

"*Signore e signori,*" he began. "Ladies and gentlemen, we apologize for the inconvenience. Our train will be delayed for several minutes." He said that he did not know how long it would be, but that he would let everyone know more in a bit. Simon picked up what words he could with the little Italian that he knew.

"The train ahead of us is probably held up," said Simon.

There were only a handful of people on the train. It was a rainy Sunday evening, and not many people were on the trains today. Simon had moved down his face to his chin and rubbed his thumb over it.

"I need to shave," he said. "I didn't shave this morning."

Claire did not look up.

"It feels good not to shave every day, though. Maybe I should grow a beard like I did last winter."

There was a long silence, and he just looked at his face. Outside, the rain was coming down at a slant, and there were streaks rolling down the window. It was the season for that kind of weather on the coast. Farther to the north, up in the mountains, there was fresh snow coming down as the clouds made their way up there from the sea.

"Look," said Claire after several minutes of silence. "I'm just trying to read this. Can you just let me read this for a while?"

Simon threw his head back against the seat. He wished he'd brought a magazine or a newspaper or something, and the train still wasn't moving. He was sitting across from Claire against the window and looked across at her.

"Hey, Claire," he said. "Where did you get that scar on your shoulder? You know the one I'm talking about? The one on your left shoulder? It looks like stitch marks. Did you get stitches there? How many?"

Claire put the magazine down with a sigh. She did not look at him. "I'm hungry," she said.

There was a woman sitting across the aisle from them eating an orange. The woman looked over when she heard Claire say this. "Do you want an orange?" she asked Claire in Italian.

"Oh, no. *Grazie*," smiled Claire with a half-smile. "No thank you."

"Go ahead, Claire," said Simon. "You like oranges."

But Claire did not move.

"You love oranges, Claire," said Simon. "Come on."

"Really," the Italian woman motioned. "It's all right. I have another one." She reached in her paper bag and pulled out another orange.

Claire didn't take it.

"Thank you," said Simon as he reached for it. "We appreciate it."

"*Prego*," said the woman.

Simon peeled the orange slowly and reached half of it out to Claire.

"No thank you," she said without lifting her eyes from the magazine.

"Go ahead," said Simon. "She gave it to you. You like oranges."

"Uh huh," she said. "But I don't want any."

Simon put half the orange in his mouth. "More for me," he mumbled through it. Claire turned and looked out the window.

A few minutes later, the train still had not moved.

"Where are we?" Claire asked, watching the drops slide down the glass.

"Just beyond Imperia," he said. "It's still a good few minutes yet. Then we have to change at Ventimiglia. We're almost to the border."

"We should have taken the car," said Claire again.

Simon pulled out his pack of cigarettes and slid each one individually up halfway out of the pack and then slid them back in. He did this twice all the way around. "Too bad they don't let you smoke on the train," he said. "Man,

they even used to let you smoke on planes. Not anymore."
He went through his cigarettes again. "You used to be able
to smoke anywhere, even in restaurants. They used to ask
you, 'Would you like smoking or non?' Can you believe
that? You can't smoke anywhere now. Not even outside
most places. They've made it a crime just about everywhere now."

He sat there for a minute watching her look at the rain
falling. No one else on the train was talking. He looked
outside, too, but there was only the dull gray sky and the
rain. It was not yet dark. He reached over for her magazine
and took it from her lap and sat there for a long time flipping through it.

"Can I look at this?" he asked a few minutes later.

She did not give any indication that she had heard him.
She only looked out the window. "What are those lights?"
she finally said, looking out toward the back of the train.

Simon looked up and turned around and saw them,
too. There were blue lights flashing, but there was no
sound. "I don't know," he said, and he turned back to the
magazine. The lights grew closer, and then a car went by
slowly toward the front of the train along the gravel on the
side of the tracks. The only sound was the tires of the car
over the stones.

"That was a police car," she said. "And I see an ambulance
back there. Maybe we hit a car. Why wasn't the siren on?"

"Nah, we didn't hit a car," said Simon without looking
up. "There isn't a cross street for another half a mile." He

flipped through the pages, back and forth, looking at the pictures but not reading. "Besides," he said, "I didn't hear or feel anything. Maybe someone on the train had a heart attack."

It had been fifteen minutes since they had stopped, and the conductor had not said anything more. A few of the passengers were starting to talk between themselves. It was getting dark outside, and the rain kept coming down.

"What are those people saying?" asked Claire. "Why haven't we moved?"

Simon was turning his way back through the magazine and did not look up. "I don't know," he said. He was now very interested in some of the pictures.

"It's getting dark," said Claire. As she said this, she saw two men walking just below her window next to the track. They were carrying flashlights and shining them along the track underneath the train. One of them was the conductor she had seen when they had boarded. He and the other man were both carrying umbrellas. They stopped just below her window and shined the flashlights underneath the train.

Before Simon knew what happened, Claire was up gathering her bags.

"What's wrong?" he asked as he looked up from the page. But before he could finish, she was already through the doors and between cars to the next one forward. All he could do was grab his things quickly and follow her.

"What the hell was that all about?" he asked when he was sitting in the seat opposite her, three cars ahead. It was the closest one to the engine.

She said nothing but leaned with her face against the window looking down. Simon saw that there were tears in her eyes and on her cheeks.

"What is..." he began. But he just sat back in his seat and said nothing. He went back to flipping through the magazine.

Ten minutes of silence later, the train jerked forward. The conductor came back on the loudspeaker. "*Signore e signori,*" he began. "We are very sorry for the inconvenience and for the delay. Our next stop will be Sanremo in approximately five minutes."

"Good, we're moving," said Simon. He looked up and across at Claire. Her eyes were nearly closed, and her cheeks were wet as she leaned her head against the glass. He could see her face in the reflection. A dark drop of rain on the outside of the window rolled down in front of her eyes, but she did not see it.

She's so high strung, this one, Simon thought to himself, looking across at her. Always getting so damn emotional over everything. What the hell's wrong with her anyway?

Letting the thought pass, he shrugged his shoulders and looked past the magazine and down at his watch. He wondered what time they would arrive in Ventimiglia for their next train.

PITCHMAN

Rick sat there in the cold wooden chair across from the reception desk, pretending to flip through the glossy documents in his folder as he did each time he was here. There were four other men seated near him, all of which he had seen there before at various times, and all in dark suits looking through their folders. He pulled out a glossy page from the middle of his folder and glanced over it, but he knew every word on the page by heart, and he knew the ins and outs of everything he would say and how he would say it. He had rehearsed it so many times. It all dealt with short-term lending notes and the most efficient cash management system a business of this size could dream of. However, it was all just a matter of getting through that door.

He heard a noise and looked up from the documents over to the secretary. So did the other men, but it was just the secretary opening a drawer and inserting some files. They all looked back down. The secretary's name was Sherri, and Rick had gotten to know her a little over the last four months. They had even gone for a brief coffee once when he had popped in without an appointment and she was on her way out to lunch. But, concerning his business, he had never made it past his seat there in the waiting room.

Six times he had received a call from Sherri just before he had left his office on his way there for an appointment. That had at least saved him the twenty-minute drive. Twice he had been turned around by a call from his own secretary on his cell phone relaying the cancellation. Five times he had made it to the office and had waited there as he did now, but then the buzzer on the desk would ring, and Sherri would pick up the phone, and then she would sadly turn to him and let him know that Mr. Allen would not be able to see him today. Rick would smile at her and thank her for her time, they would talk pleasantly for a minute or two, and then they would wave goodbye to each other knowing that they would see each other at the same time next week, which was when Sherri could next get him on the calendar.

Mr. Gregory Allen was the founder and owner of United Coatings, the largest industrial paint manufacturer and distributer in the Midwest. The company maintained its headquarters and corporate offices in a small one-story office building just outside of Madison, Wisconsin, but the major production facilities and warehouses were closer to Concord, a few miles to the east. Yet all of the money flowed through the Madison office, and so that's where Rick's services were most needed. He had learned more and more about the business over the last few months, digging up information where he could, mostly from public records and corporate profiles, and he had come to know that United Coatings was possibly sitting on seventy million dollars in cash, held at the First Mutual Bank on Bassett Street, earning exactly nine tenths of a percent per year, compounded monthly. That meant that the cash was earning just over six hundred thousand dollars per year in interest—a nice amount, to be sure, but Rick could do much better, even though interest rates were at all-time lows. The current rate Rick and his firm could offer Mr. Allen was just over 2.1 percent, which meant that the seventy million in cash could return an additional nine hundred thousand dollars per year, and it would have a far better chance of keeping up with inflation once interest rates started to pick up. This was a no-brainer to Rick and to his managers back at Regal Trust, but what drove Rick on even more was that this deal alone could earn Regal Trust an additional hundred thousand per year, of which he would get to keep slightly less than half. It meant that he could pay off his school loans sooner, move into a larger apartment closer to the center of downtown, get a new car in a few months, and in a year or two he could start thinking about settling down and starting a family. The beauty of it was, and the key to his sales pitch, was that getting the better rate did not mean that Mr. Allen would have to change his long-standing relationship with First Mutual Bank on Bassett Street, where he had been doing business for thirty-two years. Instead, it was a series of short-term lending deals that would send portions of the money out on loan for a few days at a time to large, established companies, all with triple-A credit ratings; but all the money would flow right back through First Mutual a few days later. There would always be millions of dollars available in cash on a rotating basis, allowing United Coatings' business to function as usual. But beyond this deal, there were additional opportunities for banking services, investments, retirement plans, and insurance once Rick and Regal Trust had their foot in the door. This was only the start. But it was the key to everything else.

Of course, the only problem lay in actually getting in front of Mr. Allen. Rick had given this pitch to many business owners before. He had closed deal after deal, though they had all been in the half to two million dollar range. Mr. Allen and United Coatings was Rick's big fish. It was his whale. Rick had seen Mr. Allen in person once or twice there in the office, but he had never been able to do anything more than introduce himself with a handshake before Mr. Allen dismissed him and slipped back into his office. Sherri always apologized for the way Rick was treated, but there was nothing Sherri could do to help his situation. All she could do was keep getting him back on the calendar every few weeks. Rick had grown a bit fond of Sherri during his short interactions with her. She was pretty enough, though maybe she was a few years older than him—he couldn't tell. But of course they spoke very little, and exclusively dealing with business over the phone, with a few kind words tossed in.

So, now, Rick sat there once more, watching the clock. His appointment time of two thirty had come and gone, and he knew that each minute that passed towards three o'clock he was losing his chance to get in the door that day.

Two forty came and went, and so did two forty-five. Rick glanced over at Sherri several times, but she was busy with entering something into the computer. One of the other men waiting there stood up and walked over to Sherri's desk, but all he did was grab a piece of candy from the bowl and sit back down. They all glanced often between the documents they held in their hands, their watches, and the clock on the wall. There was the ticking of the clock, the ticking of their watches, the tapping of keys on Sherri's keyboard, the irritated or nervous clearing of throats, and the turning of pages in their hands. One of the men who had arrived there before Rick got up and walked over to Sherri and spoke with her, looking at his watch.

"Should I come back tomorrow?" the man asked. "My appointment was at one."

Sherri nodded. She looked down at her calendar and flipped through it. "I can get you in next Wednesday," she said. "Same time? One o'clock?"

"Sure, sure," said the man. "All right. Thank you."

He came back to his chair, grabbed his coat and his leather folder, and went out the door into the cool autumn air.

Rick felt the breeze come in and move across his face. It chilled him a little. He looked at his watch and saw it was two fifty-two. He knew he wasn't going to get in today, but he also knew that he'd wait there another hour or two just in case there was an opening. He had cleared his afternoon of any other appointments, as he always did on days when he was supposed to meet with Mr. Allen.

Three o'clock nervously came and went, and it was soon approaching three twenty. Two of the other men had left, and it was now just Rick, one other man, and Sherri there in the room. Hesitantly, Rick got up and walked over to Sherri's desk and picked up a piece of candy from the bowl. He unwrapped it and stuck it in his mouth.

"Hi Sherri," said Rick. "D'you think I'll get in there today?"

Sherri looked down at her calendar. "Two thirty, huh?" she said. "Probably not today. Should I reschedule you?"

Rick turned the piece of candy over in his mouth and sucked on it a few times. "Hmm," he said, "I'll wait just a bit longer, I guess. I moved all my other appointments for today, so I can just wait a bit longer, if you don't mind."

"Not at all," laughed Sherri. "Maybe he'll have a few free minutes later. He's still meeting with his ten o'clock, if you can believe it. They haven't even had a break for lunch!"

Rick looked at the clock and widened his eyes for effect. "Well," said Rick, "guess I'll wait a bit then."

"Sure," said Sherri. "Maybe you want to wait over here instead of over there. I'm done with all the purchase order requests I had to file."

Rick looked back at the chair he had been sitting in, his folder of glossy pitch materials sitting over there, and the other man who looked like he was starting to get sleepy. Then he turned and saw the upholstered chair a few feet from Sherri's desk. "All right," he said as he pulled it up next to her desk. "If you don't mind."

"No," said Sherri. "Of course not."

Rick didn't know what to say at first. He started with some pleasantries, but he knew very little about Sherri or where to begin. Their conversations usually stuck to finding a mutually convenient meeting time. "Got any vacations coming up?" he asked her, his voice almost cracking.

Sherri shrugged her shoulders and shook her head. "Nope," she said. "Not until after the New Year. Gotta spend Thanksgiving and Christmas here with the family, of course. But maybe in the spring or summer. I don't have anything planned yet."

Rick shook his head. He said that he had the same plan.

"Where are you thinking of going?" asked Sherri.

Rick pulled something out of thin air. "Australia," he said. "A friend of mine back in the office went with his wife a few months ago for their tenth anniversary. They loved it, and they said I should go sometime. They went to Sydney and Melbourne, and they absolutely loved the trip."

"You're gonna go with your wife or girlfriend?" asked Sherri.

Rick waved his hand and dismissed the idea. "Oh, no," he said. "I'm not married or anything, remember?"

Sherri blushed a little. They had spoken a little over coffee the one time, but she hadn't remembered if he were married or not. That was a month or two ago. "So you're gonna go on your own, then?" she asked.

Rick shrugged his shoulders. "Maybe. Or maybe I'll go with a friend or something."

"Sounds nice. I've never been to Australia. I've been to Puerto Rico once, a few years ago. But I've never been as far away as Australia."

"Yeah?" said Rick. "How was that? In Puerto Rico?"

"Oh, it was pretty nice. Hot and sunny, and the water was really warm. It felt like bath water. A group of us went to one of those all-inclusive resorts."

"That's pretty nice," said Rick. "I've never been to Puerto Rico, or anywhere down there. Just to Orlando once. Disney World and all. Didn't make it to the beach, though."

"Yeah," said Sherri. "I haven't been to Disney World, but I've been to Disneyland in California. That's the one in California, right? Disneyland?"

"Uh huh. I think so."

"Well, that's where we went on a family vacation once, when I was ten. It was fun, I guess, from what I remember. We drove all the way there."

"That's neat," said Rick. He didn't have much else to say. He searched his brain for something to keep the conversation going, and he dreaded the silence that might come and make it awkward. "Brothers or sisters?" he asked her.

"Two brothers and two sisters. You?"

"One brother and two sisters," said Rick.

They went on like this for a few minutes, and that was enjoyable, thought Rick. But he knew that he wanted to try to insert something about the deal he was trying to propose. He had mentioned it briefly when they'd had coffee a few weeks before, when Sherri had asked him what he did and why he wanted to meet with Mr. Allen, but Rick had only spoken hurriedly about it. He had only mentioned the key points, just in case Sherri might be able to drop a sentence or two with Mr. Allen and pass on the importance of the meeting to him. Finally, when there was a pause in the conversation, he went ahead and asked her outright, though he was uneasy doing so.

"Hey, Sherri," he said, "did you ever mention anything to Mr. Allen about why I wanted to meet with him?" He tried to say this in a way so that he didn't come across too businesslike. He wanted things to remain friendly between them, as he knew Sherri was the key to getting in to see Mr. Allen. She was the key to this whole deal, in fact. If he remained on good terms with her, only then would he eventually be able to get through that door.

"Uh huh," she said. "About a week or two ago, before the last time you were here. I was going through the list of appointments, and he asked what you were on the calendar for. I said that you were from Regal Trust and that you could make the company more money on its idle cash. I didn't remember exactly what you told me, but that's what I said to him. He paused for several seconds, and then he told me to keep you on the schedule and not to turn you away yet."

Rick nearly jumped out of his seat as he heard this. His heart leapt, and he felt a bit lightheaded. He tried not to show any emotion. "Good, good," he said. "Thank you for mentioning that. That will help me. It certainly will help the company earn more on its cash." But he didn't want to discuss too much more with her. "Thank you for doing that, Sherri," he said. "I appreciate it."

She nodded. "You're welcome. I really do think he wants to meet with you. It's just that he does everything with First Mutual. We have a CFO here, but Mr. Allen still handles a lot of the banking stuff. Plus he never sticks to his appointment schedule."

"No, of course not," said Rick. He thought about the dozen failed appointments so far. But now he immediately wanted to get back to more friendly conversation and away from business. He didn't want to trouble Sherri with shop talk if he could avoid it. But he was glad to know that she had made mention of him to Mr. Allen. "So," he said, "where did you go to school? Here in Madison?"

Again the conversation turned more personal, and Rick learned that Sherri was twenty-six and was actually three years younger than him. She was a Badger and had graduated here in Madison with a degree in Marketing and a minor in Journalism, but she had taken the job for Mr. Allen because her family had always been close to his family. There were even two marriages between their families, somewhere along the line. Rick talked a little about himself, but he kept turning the questions back to her, as he knew he should. He didn't want her to know how boring his life was.

Several minutes later, the last remaining man from the waiting room came over to the desk.

"Can you reschedule me?" he asked Sherri. "I was his one thirty."

Sherri turned back to her calendar and found him a new timeslot a week and a half away that worked for him. He traveled on the road a lot, and he would only be back this way for a few days that week. His company was a distributor of industrial lubricants, and Rick could see that he was trying to position himself as the main supplier for the production facilities in Concord. Once the meeting was set, the man smiled at her, and then at Rick, and then he grabbed his things and walked out the door. As he did so, another man walked in and came up to the desk without taking his coat off.

"Hello," the man said. "I'm here for my four o'clock appointment with Mr. Allen."

Sherri looked up at the clock. It was three fifty. "Certainly, Mr. Edwards," she said, looking at her calendar. "You can have a seat if you'd like. I can tell you that Mr. Allen is several hours behind in his meetings today. He may not be able to see you right at four. But then he has to be out of the office at five for a flight. You can certainly wait if you'd like."

The man considered this for a moment. "Hmm," he said, "do you think I should reschedule?"

Sherri grinned apologetically. "Yeah, probably."

The man smiled with a sigh, but Rick saw that he was not really upset. This had happened many times before, just as it had with all of them.

"I'm sorry, Mr. Edwards," she said. She looked at her calendar. "I can get you in next Thursday if you'd like. Ten o'clock in the morning?"

"Sure," said the man. "Ten o'clock would be fine. Thank you." He nodded and left the desk, then he was out the door again.

That left Rick and Sherri alone in the office there. There was only silence and the ticking of the clock on the wall for a minute or two. Periodically they could hear muffled voices in Mr. Allen's office behind them through the frosted glass door, but mostly it was quiet. Rick casually pushed his chair an inch away from the desk, just in case Mr. Allen came out and saw him socializing with his secretary. He tried not to let Sherri notice.

"He's leaving at five?" asked Rick.

"Uh huh," said Sherri. "Flight to Houston."

Rick nodded. "D'you think I'll get in at all today?"

Sherri shook her head. "No, probably not."

There were a few more moments of silence between them. Rick was about to get up.

"But," said Sherri, "you can wait around a bit longer if you'd like, just in case. I'm not kicking you out or anything."

"All right," smiled Rick. "I'll stay a bit longer if you don't mind. It's either that or just head back to the office and do some paperwork."

"Would you like some coffee?"

Rick didn't drink coffee very much. He didn't like the taste. But he knew he wouldn't turn down the offer. "Sure," he said. "Thank you."

Sherri got up and walked over to the coffee pot. Rick watched her hips sway as she stepped in her heels. She was not the most attractive woman he had ever known, but she was fairly pretty. There was something about her that he knew he liked. "Cream and sugar?" she asked.

"No," said Rick. "Just black is all right."

She came back with a cup for him and one for herself. The cups had the company logo on them in blue. Rick took a small sip of the bitter black liquid that burned his lips and muscled it down without wincing.

"A little hot," said Sherri.

"It's ok," said Rick. "It's good."

At four fifteen they paused as they heard yelling coming from inside the office. They waited, perhaps for the door to open, but nothing happened. It was Mr. Allen's voice.

"He yells sometimes," said Sherri. "It's pretty funny. Not often, but he'll yell sometimes over the littlest things. The paper in the copier's the wrong shade of white, the sales numbers from Iowa are on the wrong form, the manager at Concord won't answer the phone. It's actually quite funny watching him, because he's such a little man." She whispered these last few sentences so that her voice could not be heard inside.

At four thirty, Sherri got up and poured him another cup of coffee. Rick stood up from his chair and took another piece of candy from the bowl. Then the conversation went to plans about the future. Rick said he was fairly happy with Regal Trust and saw himself becoming the branch manager one day. Sherri talked about getting her master's degree in business and then working for Mr. Allen in their accounting department, or maybe working for another company in Madison or Milwaukee, but not as far away as Chicago. She had no definite plans.

At four fifty-three, Rick finally looked at his watch with some apathy. "Well," he sighed, "I should probably get out of here and get out of your hair. I'm sure I'm keeping you from work."

"Oh, I don't mind," said Sherri. "I enjoyed having you here to keep me company. You don't have to go if you don't want to."

"It's ok," said Rick. "I really should go. Doesn't Mr. Allen have to leave right at five?"

"Yeah, he does."

"All right," said Rick, "I'll just grab my things and my coat, if you don't mind finding me a new appointment time. I'm available whenever. I'll make time. Any day is fine."

Sherri turned to her calendar, and Rick walked over and grabbed his folder. He started putting on his coat.

"And thank you again for the coffee...," Rick began. But as he said this, the door to Mr. Allen's office opened. Mr. Allen, a very short, bald man with bushy white eyebrows, was thanking the man he had been meeting with and was shaking his hand vigorously.

"So I'll see you in Chicago then?" the man asked Mr. Allen.

"Fine, fine," said Mr. Allen. "Chicago. On the fifteenth."

"Yes," said the man. "The fifteenth."

"Write that down, Sherri," said Mr. Allen. "I'll need a car to Chicago on the morning of the fifteenth. I don't want to fly this time—I hate those little prop planes. I'd rather just take a car and avoid all the security and everything. That way I can work on the road."

"Yes, Mr. Allen," said Sherri as she wrote everything down.

Mr. Allen then saw Rick near the door putting on his jacket.

"Who's this?" he asked Sherri.

"It's Mr. Lyle," said Sherri. "From Regal Trust. He was your two thirty."

Mr. Allen looked at Rick as he stood there with his coat half on. Then he looked at his watch. "You're a bit late then, aren't you?" said Mr. Allen.

Rick looked at Sherri with a blank stare. Neither of them knew what to say or how to answer Mr. Allen.

"Well," said Mr. Allen, "you've got exactly five minutes and then I've got to be on my way to the airport. But five minutes and no more." Then he said goodbye to the man who was on his way out and went back into his office with the door left open.

Rick scrambled to get his jacket off and reached down to grab his folder with all the glossy pitch pieces. They nearly fell out as he did so, but he caught them and slid them back in. Sherri saw this and smiled. Rick walked briskly toward the door, but Sherri jumped up from her chair and stood in front of him.

"Hold on!" she said. She reached up and grabbed Rick's collar, which was standing up against the back of his neck from removing his coat. Then she patted down his lapels and straightened his tie. "You look good," she said with a smile. Rick could smell her perfume and look into her eyes so close there. He had never smelled her perfume before. It was subtle and flowery. "Good luck in there," she whispered.

"Thanks," said Rick nervously. "Thank you." And he walked into the office and pulled the door shut behind him.

At five thirty that evening, when Rick returned to his office and started settling back in behind his desk, the branch manager and another manager visiting from Milwaukee came into his office and stood at the door.

"Close the deal?" Rodney, the branch manager, laughed. He knew Rick had never even met with Mr. Allen yet.

Rick sat back in his seat and took a deep breath. "Not yet," he said with a half-smile. "But I got in there today. I actually got to talk with him for a few minutes. Told him about the cash deal and the better rate. He liked it. He nodded and said 'Yes, yes' a lot. It was progress."

"So," said Jeff, the other manager, "you think you can close it?"

"I think so. Got another meeting with him next Thursday," said Rick. "I showed him the papers to sign today—got right to the point—but he was on his way to the airport. He said I should bring everything back with me at our next meeting, and not to rush into signing paperwork. He won't agree to anything until he has time to look through all the details, but I think he sees the benefit. Doesn't even want to get the CFO involved, since he likes to handle all this stuff on his own. He said he never goes in big with anything. He's got to start small and see what we can do for him before he'll commit to anything more. A trial run, you know? Let's us at least get in there a bit. I told him we'd be fine with that. We'd go as slow as he wants."

"So," said Rodney, "you need one of us to come along? Help you close it? We won't even take a cut if we get it. We just want to get the deal done, for your sake."

Rick looked at both of them. "No, no," he said. He knew they'd both get their share anyways, since they were managers inside his region. And he knew he could handle it on his own. "I've got this," he said. "But thank you."

"You know we've all tried to get him before," said Rodney. "No one's ever been able to get in front of him for more than a few minutes, let alone close it. I tried two years ago. Jeff here tried before that when he was here in this office."

Rick nodded.

"All right," said Jeff. "Well hopefully next Thursday you can get it done. Thursday, right?"

"Yeah."

They both came over and shook his hand.

"Good night," they both said. "We're off to the Blues game tonight. Got free tickets just yesterday."

"Nice!" said Rick. "Good night then."

He sat there for a while longer. Everyone else in the office was gone, including all the administrative staff. He knew he would have to lock up. Since the Blues were playing, they had all cut out early. He sat there and thought about everything he had said in the five minutes he'd had with Mr. Allen. He repeated everything over in his mind. He had been flawless. This was his whale, and he had hit him with every main point perfectly. Instead of thirty minutes, he had laid everything out in less than five. There was no way he wouldn't get this deal. All he had to do was get through that door one more time and get a solid twenty minutes or so with Mr. Allen to go through all the details. Sherri would be able to make that happen for him. He was glad he had stayed and chatted with her.

At around six o'clock, just as he was about to lock up after preparing for his meetings the next day, the phone on his desk rang.

"Hello? Rick Lyle," he answered.

"Hello, Rick," said the woman's voice on the other end. "It's Sherri Peck at Mr. Allen's office." She paused, waiting for Rick's response.

"Yes, hi, Sherri," said Rick. "How are you?"

"I'm good," she said. "I'm glad I caught you before you left. Do you have a minute?"

"Sure, of course." He sat down on the edge of his desk.

"Okay. Mr. Allen called me from the airport and said that he wants to change your appointment with him."

Rick scoffed into the phone, and then caught himself and hoped Sherri hadn't heard. He had heard this too many times, and he had just told Rodney and Jeff about the meeting next Thursday.

"Mr. Allen wants to fly back early from Houston tomorrow afternoon," Sherri continued, "and he wants to meet with you tomorrow night. Is that all right with you?"

Rick smiled to himself. "Sure!" he said. "What time?"

Sherri hesitated. "Seven o'clock tomorrow evening," she said. "Is that too late for you? I can always tell him..."

Rick laughed. "No, no, not at all! I'll meet with him at any time. Tomorrow at seven is perfect."

"You're sure?" asked Sherri.

"Of course. That'll definitely work."

"Good," said Sherri. "I already told him that was fine for you. He said he'll be here, and he's bringing the CFO into the meeting as well, just to hammer out all the details."

Rick's heart pounded. This was his big one, his big break. If he could close this deal tomorrow, that would set him up pretty well. But he also didn't want to get too excited. Mr. Allen had the bad habit of rescheduling, and he'd already said that he wanted to start small, if at all. Rick wouldn't get his hopes up too much. Not yet, anyway.

"Good," said Rick. "Thank you, Sherri. That's great news. Thank you."

"All right," said Sherri. "Seven o'clock tomorrow then. Here at the office."

"Of course. Thank you."

Then there were several moments of silence on the phone. Neither of them wanted to say goodbye. Rick thought about seeing Sherri up close and smelling her perfume. Sherri eventually broke the silence.

"Rick?" she asked. "Are you going to the Blues game tonight?"

"Oh, no," said Rick. "I was just about to head home. Why? Are you going?"

"Well, I was," said Sherri. "But then my friend Rachel called me and said she couldn't make it."

Rick was silent for a moment. "And, so…," he began.

"My parents have tickets to all the home games," said Sherri. "Do you like hockey games?"

Rick laughed into the phone. "Of course!" he said. He actually wasn't much of a hockey fan, but he had been to a few Blues games. He would certainly endure a game with Sherri if he could. It sure as hell beat the cardboard pizza he would pull out of the freezer and the four or five bottles of cheap beer he would drink tonight while watching TV before he fell asleep. He'd rather drink cheap beer and eat junk food at a hockey game with a cute girl like Sherri.

"Okay, good," said Sherri. "Would you want to go there with me tonight? I want to go, but I don't want to go alone."

"Absolutely!" said Rick. "I'd love to."

"Good," said Sherri. "Should I meet you at the arena? It's out on Pleasant View Road. You know where that is?"

"Of course, of course," said Rick. "I can head there right now, or I could pick you up on my way."

"Oh, no," said Sherri. "You were just out here. It's pretty far out of your way. I'll meet you at the arena."

"All right," said Rick. He was glad she wouldn't have to ride in his car. "You should give me your cell phone number, just in case."

"Okay. Sure."

She gave him the number, and then he dialed it so that she had his, too.

"All right, then," said Rick. "I'll see you there in about a half an hour?" He looked at his watch and noted the time.

"Sounds good," said Sherri. "I'll see you then."

Rick hung up the phone and smiled to himself. He wasn't sure if he were happier about the meeting being moved to tomorrow or about the hockey game and seeing Sherri. What he did know was that he wouldn't have more than one or two beers, and that he didn't want Rodney or Jeff or anyone else from the office to see him there with Sherri. Someone might say something about Mr. Allen or about the deal to mess it all up for him, one way or the other. He would have to keep his eyes open and be on his toes. It was best not to see anyone from the office there, or at least just say hi and keep moving.

Rick locked up the office and got into his car out in the parking lot. It was nearly freezing. The car was ten years old when he had bought it, and that was four years ago. He was able to get it to start on the third crank. He thought about the deal and about how he'd be able to get a loan for a brand new car once everything was signed and the first commission check hit. That might be a month or two away yet, but he could wait. He'd kept the car running so far.

He pulled out of the parking lot and into traffic. The night was cool and crisp, and he could see several stars in the open black sky above. The Doobie Brothers were coming through with static on the radio, and the warm air from the defroster and the cool air from the window that wouldn't stay up mixed to feel relatively pleasant. It settled into his mind that he was actually on his way to a date tonight. He had not been on a date in several months, as work took up all of his time lately, and he didn't have much excitement to offer any of the girls who worked downtown. He was just trying to survive making little deals here and there, just to pay the bills and stay ahead of everything. He rarely had time to enjoy himself these days. He barely had any time to breathe.

But maybe, just possibly, that was all about to change.

GINGER

Hell, I've got it bad for Ginger, but she's the only one I can't have. Eight hundred thousand women on this god damn island, last I counted, and Ginger's gotta be off limits. Well, maybe that's for the best. If anything ever happened, I'm sure I'd just blow it all up. Still, I've got it pretty bad for her. There's no way 'round that. She's the only girl in Manhattan worth a damn.

Ginger's got that flamin' red hair. Tall glass of water, too. And thin. Looks just like that girl the Professor was shaggin' on that show. Only worn out and beat up a bit from life. This girl's seen more than anyone ever should see. She's just worn out. Been workin' since she was ten. Got a real name, I'm sure. Used to know it. Cynthia maybe.

Hell, I don't know. But then I started callin' her Ginger, and it just stuck. Everyone calls her Ginger now, even Ben. And she's even gotten to the point where she calls herself that now, too. It fits, you know. And she's pretty much the only girl I want to be with. No one gets me like Ginger, and I think I'm the only one that really gets her. Not even Ben gets her the way I do. Talkin' to her is just right to me. Like listenin' to that slow jazz on a record player, with just a piano and a bass and a low, slow trumpet. And maybe that brush on the snare in the background. Yeah, just like that slow, steady brush on the snare. It's just right. You feel safe with her. Like when we catch a smoke together out back, or when she laughs at one of my bad jokes and puts her hands on me. She's the only woman I've ever cared about. But, of course, I can't have her the way I want her. I know it'd just ruin it. It's my own rule, and I've gotta stick to it.

Ginger is Ben's girl, and Ben's my cousin. Don't know that for sure that he's my cousin, but we think so. Grew up together, our families did, and always used to call his dad Uncle Ben. Ben owns Benny's. Just like his dad Ben did. Just like his dad. All down the line. Benjamin James, Benjamin Jacob, Benjamin J. Harding, one after another. Ben's number seven I think. No way to know for sure. But they've had this place a long time. Been comin' here even since before I was born. When mom was pregnant she would come with my dad and drink and smoke. Back then it wasn't bad for you. But all our parents are dead and gone now, so it's just Ben and me. We're the only family left.

He's pretty much adopted me since he's older. Five years. Even though I'm grown now. Actually, even back in the day Ben used to get the hell beat out of him and I used to have to save his sorry ass. He was always smaller'n me. People say we look like brothers. I don't think so. We don't even look alike. I'm tall and have all my hair, and he's short and bald. At thirty. Lost it all before he was nineteen, can you believe that?

Ben lets me work behind the bar when I want. Been doin' it since I was fourteen. Half the time I'm behind the bar, the other half the time I'm in front of it. He also lets me sleep there up above. There's room enough, and I've cut out my own little space and put up some plywood. There're two rooms and a shower. We use the bathroom downstairs in the bar. Two separate rooms and enough thickness in the walls in case I bring a girl up with me. He doesn't mind. Neither does Ginger. At least they never say anything. We just kick the girls out in the morning when we have to unload a shipment of bottles and restock the bar. But if the girl hangs around too much we tell her she's not welcome anymore. Private property and all that. I'm in front of the bar whenever I have money. Ben understands that. I only work when I can't afford to pay for drinks—then I drink for free. And the people love me there, too. There's a big group of locals that hangs out there still, and they all know us and love it when I'm workin' there. Not good tips, ya know, but a good time anyway. Pretty good gig.

Only problem with bein' related to Ben is Ginger. I made a rule long ago never to mess with Ben. He's the only family I've got. I've stolen girls from everyone else. Hell, my friends don't bring their girls around me anymore. Don't have any morals—can't afford them. But not from Ben. Ben's blood. He puts a roof over my head. Sure, Ginger and I joke about runnin' off together, right in front of Ben even. But I'd never do that to him. I'd never do that to myself. Ruin everything, I'm sure.

So I end up at Benny's tonight and Ben sees me and the question in his eye is which side of the bar I'll be on. It's a Saturday afternoon and the place is packed, and it looks like he needs help anyway, so I step behind the bar.

The place is packed and I wash up and start takin' orders and pullin' bottles before Ben and I have a chance to say more than "hey." This back alley place used to be a local joint, but now it's been taken over by yups and champagne communists. The yups are the worst, only because they're so damn noisy. The Reds are all right. We locals keep comin' because Ben's great and because change is hard. The prices doubled when the yuppies moved in, but the local discount kept the prices for the rest of us the same. Not too many locals left here anymore. Just a few of us left. Damn yuppies've taken over the whole damn island.

When Ben and I both reach for the register at once, we finally get a chance to talk.

"Hey, man. Long time," he says with a punch to my shoulder.

I ask Ben if Scott's there and he says he's not. Ben tells me it's because there's a new clerk at the liquor store he works at, and he's droolin' all over her. Ben hasn't seen him since soon after she started workin' there. Scott's been workin' every shift he can, he says, even weekends, just to see her. It's always that way. We never see Scott when he's hot on a girl. He 'specially won't bring her 'round me. He's learned. It's happened too many times. But good for Scott. Anyway, that doesn't get me a drink, so when I have a free minute I pour myself one, and I know Ben doesn't mind. He never does. Big sip of whisky while I mix a fruity drink for some yup and his yup girlfriend.

While the whisky's still burnin' my eyes, I see Ginger comin' down the stairs in slow motion with her tray like some scene in a movie, and she winks at me and I wave back. Tight faded jeans and a real low-cut top. Still stuck in the eighties. She'd wear leg warmers if she could get away with it. Always gets me feelin' good when I see her. From that far away, she's just as pretty as any girl anywhere in the world. There're a few tables upstairs, and Ginger comes over to me behind the bar with a whole list order for me to pour and kisses me on the cheek. I turn and catch the side of her mouth.

"You sly dog," she smiles as she pinches my cheek.

Ben sees us and just shakes his head. When I turn back, Ginger's gone again.

It's just an hour or two later and the sun's comin' in low through the windows from a building out on Second

Avenue. The whole evening flies by since it's so packed and no one leaves but new groups keep comin' in. Around nine it starts to get real rowdy and I feel like takin' a break out back so my ears get a rest. Everyone's tryin' to shout over each other and I haven't had a free second since I got there. But before I get a chance to step out, this girl I'm servin' turns from the bar and spills her drink on some guy standin' behind her. Well, he starts raisin' a fuss, and then the girl's boyfriend steps in and starts raisin' a fuss, and before anyone can say anything Ben and I are out from behind the bar and drag one of the guys out front. Damn yups. Always gotta raise a fuss.

Well, no one likes a fight in a crowded bar, and so Ben tells the guy to move along.

"But my girlfriend's in there!" the guy says. He's a big tough guy. Big fat face. But he's wearin' skinny jeans that make me laugh.

"That's not my problem," says Ben. "You're not going back in."

"Aw, come on. I'll play nice." He tries to push his way back in.

"Nope," says Ben flatly. "I'll call the cops."

I'm just there for moral support. Ben can handle himself. I'm busy lightin' a cigarette tryin' to catch a quick smoke.

So this guy steps away to the curb and starts cussin' and pulls out his cell phone and calls his chick. As Ben and I walk back in, the girl shuffles through the crowd past us to leave. Damn yups. They got the money, though, so without them there'd be no Benny's. Ben can charge them ten-up on a beer and they don't even blink. Crazy.

It's the busiest I've ever seen the place and that night I make a good three hondo in tips. Usually when things are slow you gotta send the collection plate around again, but not tonight. I'll give Ginger a hundred and keep two for myself. Tax free. Uncle Sam ain't touchin' any of this money. Far as Uncle Sam knows, I don't even exist. I'm as free as you can get. Livin' the dream. Two hundred'll last me all week. I've got no bills—just goes straight to my pocket. I don't even have an ID card, let alone a bank account. I'm small fry to Uncle Sam. Just a few ink marks on a sheet of paper in a warehouse somewhere. Doesn't even know I exist.

It's almost two in the morning by the time things cool down enough for me to step outside for a smoke. It's warm out, but cooler than inside. Halfway down my cigarette Ginger comes out and pulls some grass from her pocket and pulls my cigarette from my mouth and tosses it to the ground. Ben doesn't smoke anything, so Ginger and I smoke together anything we can find. Ben hates that she smokes. I'm leanin' with my back to the wall and Ginger pins me against the wall with her hips and her tits and brings her face close to mine so that I can feel the sweat comin' off her and smell her perfume. I pause for a second, then lean forward to try and kiss her on the mouth, but then she turns her head away laughin' and slips the joint in my mouth.

"Light this," she says.

Damn, I hate when she does that. Always messes me up.

So we bend down sittin' against the wall next to each other passin' it between us, not talkin' much.

"You're way too good lookin' for Ben," I finally say to her.

"Yeah, I know," she says. "When you hit the lottery, we'll run away together."

"Never bought a ticket."

"Well, hard to win then, isn't it? This could all be yours." She runs her hand from her tits down to her ass.

Damn, I think to myself. Now she's just messin' with me. Always messin' with me.

A minute later, she's on the topic of reincarnation. Ginger's one of these New Age types. Studyin' Chinese medicine or something. Burns incense and rings little bells and what not. Might get her out from behind the bar someday anyway. I tell her it's all black magic, but she laughs and says that a lot of it has been proven by Western medicine. Sure it has.

"Well you're not stickin' any pins in me," I say.

"Noted."

"Not unless you get naked first."

"Deal."

She takes a long pull from the joint and coughs low.

"You back for good?" she asks me.

I'd spent a few nights away, shackin' up with some girl I met. "Sure," I say. "Realized I just couldn't live without you. Had to come back."

"Ripe," she says. "Some little princess kick you to the curb?"

"Nah," I say.

She knows I'm lyin'.

"Good for you," she says. "You gonna call up Bridgette again?"

"You mean Yoko?" I ask as I blow the smoke out slowly. "Nah. Don't like Asians so much anymore. Why? Has she come 'round lookin' for me?"

"Just once," says Ginger. "A few days ago. She looked pretty upset."

"Ah, she'll be all right."

Ginger takes another drag. "Ben said the other day he missed you."

"Wow, that's a big step. I didn't know Ben had any feelings."

"Sure he does," she says. "Ben's soft as a marshmallow inside. You never see it, though. I've even seen him cry."

"Doubt it."

"Sure I have."

"What, you got him goin' to therapy or somethin'?"

"Something like that."

We're silent for a minute or two. I take a last long drag on the joint as the heavy rusted steel door opens and Ben pokes his face out. He sees me holdin' it in and rolls his eyes at Ginger. She just shrugs her shoulders with a smile.

"Last group is gone," he says. "I'm gonna close up."

"All right," says Ginger. "We'll be right in."

She and I stand up and wipe our backs off from the wall. I help wipe her back off and spend some extra time rubbin' her ass until she figures out what I'm doin' and starts gigglin'.

"All right, you perv. That's enough."

She loves it, though.

"So what are you gonna come back as?" I ask her. "When you get reincarnated?"

"I don't know," she says. "A parrot maybe. Maybe a cat. Or a grasshopper."

"Well," I say, "I'm gonna come back as a killer whale."

"A killer whale?"

"Sure. Why not?"

"Who's a killer whale?" asks Ben as we step in and he's closin' up the register.

"Aw, never mind," I say. "Nothin'." It was meant for Ginger, not for Ben.

Ginger just laughs.

The bar is so quiet without anyone there. It feels so empty. The silence is louder than the yellin'. The whole place smells like dry, sticky beer, and we'll have to scrub everything down tomorrow, not just the tables.

A few minutes later, they're startin' to walk upstairs with a pair of beers to go to bed.

"You stayin' here tonight?" Ben asks me.

I'm pullin' up a bottle from behind the bar for a sip. "Nah, I've got the key though. Thought I might go out lookin' for some trouble."

Ben just shakes his head. "All right. Maybe see you in the morning then. Delivery at seven."

Ginger blows me a kiss.

I answer with a nod as he shuts off the lights.

Out on the street I light up a cigarette and start walkin' uptown. Then I think better of it and cross over Second and head down toward Forty-Fifth.

"Somethin' good'll be open," I say. "Gonna find something good downtown."

I shake my head, but all I can think about is Ginger's hips against mine and the smell of her sweat mixed with her perfume. Good stuff.

Up ahead I see a shop that's open twenty-four hours and feel the roll of cash in my pocket. Thinkin' 'bout how fast I can spend it. I stop in and buy a pack of cigarettes— and a lottery ticket. Never played before.

"What numbers you want?" the Paki guy asks me.

"What?"

"Numbers? What numbers?" He's in a hurry for some reason, but I'm the only one in there.

"Hell, I don't know," I say. "Whatever. Just make 'em good ones. Throw a seven in there. Seven's lucky, right?"

I take my ticket and look at it, then shove it in my pocket. I put a cigarette between my lips as I head out the door.

"Maybe I'll win," I laugh under my breath.

Hell. Maybe I will.

SUGARLOAF KEY

Lionel left the house in his shorts through the screen door and walked down toward the beach facing south toward the open flats. The heartburn was making it so he couldn't sleep these last few nights. Sure, the doc had given him some pills, but they weren't helping much. So he got up and left Mariah sleeping in the bed and went outside. Once there, the warm, humid air felt good on his skin and on his bare chest, and with the light breeze coming from the southeast there would be no mosquitoes out. Mullet were jumping in the shallows, and the slap of their bodies against the water told him the flats were alive in the silence despite the fact that everyone living on the shore was asleep. Even standing there on the beach, the slow lapping of the waves at high tide added only the slightest sound to the night.

High up above, the full moon shone brightly in the cloudless sky. Only far off to the south were any clouds visible, and they were only low gray wisps along the horizon. The moon shone down and lit up the night as if it were daytime. In an attempt to pass half an hour or so until he grew tired, and without any real aim of catching anything, Lionel grabbed an old spinning rod off the dock, put a bait on, and threw it into the water. The line had no weight on it but only a 3/0 hook, which was perfect for the small greenbacks he found still alive in the bait bucket hanging in the water from one of the pilings. He hooked one through the back near the tail and tossed it as far out onto the flats as he could.

Resting on the beach was an old weathered pine log that had washed up a few days before. It looked like part of a telephone pole, except that it wasn't treated. He'd thought he might find a use for it and had pulled it up on shore, and now it made a perfect seat just a few feet from the water. Within five minutes of sitting, he had a fish on and reeled in a ten-inch mangrove snapper, fighting it to shore without having to get up. But he threw it back and reached into the bait bucket for another greenback before throwing the line out again. He sat there for several minutes, and this time there were no bites. So he sat there and looked out toward the water and listened to the mullet jumping in the shallows just offshore, trying to feel sleepy again.

Far out across the flats he saw a bright light scanning the water. It was a searchlight from a boat. The light passed from his left along the shore, over him, and on to the right. Maybe it had been out there all along, thought Lionel, but only now did he notice it. He watched the light, and he saw that the boat it was attached to was making its way westward toward Saddlebunch.

"Just fishing?" he asked himself aloud. But he saw the light continue to scan the shore and the water all around. "Nah, they're definitely looking for something," he said.

He sat there for a while and watched, not feeling any tugs on his line. The light was always there, scanning the water and the shore, but the boat moved into and out of his view several times as it made its way back and forth on the water. He couldn't tell what type of boat it was, but it looked to him like it might be a small Coast Guard or police boat because of all the lights on it.

"What're they doing here?" he asked himself. "Haven't seen the Coast Guard around here much lately." He usually saw the Coast Guard vessels a few miles west near Boca Chica around the Naval Air Station. But he didn't think too much of it and turned back to his fishing line. He wondered if there were still a bait at the end, and so he started to reel it in slowly.

But far out on the water, there came sounds from the boat. The searchlight had fixed itself on something in the water to his left out of view. The engines came up, the boat made a quick U-turn and came up to speed, and the loudspeaker was shouting something in Spanish. The boat rocketed forward and out of sight.

"Hmm," was all Lionel said.

By now the line was in, and he saw that the greenback was still on it and still wiggling. He pulled the rod back behind him and swung the bait out again, all without getting up from the log. Then he threw the bail of the reel over and waited.

A minute or so later, he heard a noise over to his right, just beyond his small, rickety dock extending out from the beach.

"Something in the water," he said. "Snook, maybe. Or maybe tarpon."

But the splashes grew stronger, and a moment later a small aluminum boat came into view. There were several men in it, all sitting very low in the boat and paddling over the side with oars. There was a small engine on the back of the boat, but it was not running and had been tilted up.

"What the…?" he began.

Then, all of a sudden, there was a series of loud splashes, and he saw that the men had all rolled over the sides of the boat and were now swimming wildly toward his beach. There was a mad dash as they all swam the last twenty yards to the shore.

Lionel sat there just watching them, not afraid, but more confused than anything.

When the men had made it up onto shore, they all collapsed there on the sand, shouting loud words to each other that Lionel did not understand. He shifted his seat on the log and sat there watching them curiously from only a few feet away.

"Hmm," Lionel said to himself again. "What the hell's this all about?" But as soon as he said this, it all clicked in his mind. "Ahh," he said. "Cubans." Then he laughed to himself. "Well, guess those bastards made it." He listened in the distance and could hear the Coast Guard boat shouting something in Spanish, but he didn't see the searchlight anymore. Lionel didn't move. He just sat there and watched the men. They were now sitting up on the sand in a small group talking quietly. A moment later, one of them noticed him sitting there on the log and stood up quickly. Lionel watched as they started over toward him, all with their hands high above their heads, saying words he did not understand.

"Por favor!" said the one nearest him. He was a short man with grease-stained khaki slacks on and a red flannel shirt, soaking wet. He must be their leader, Lionel thought. *"Policía?"* the man asked.

"What's that?" Lionel replied.

"Policía!" the man said again. *"Comprende? Policía?"*

"Huh?" Lionel did not know what the man was saying. "Hey look, guys," he said, "I don't speak no Spanish. Do any of you all speak any English?"

"Inglés?" asked the man. He looked around to his buddies. They all shook their heads. *"No,"* he said. *"No Inglés."* Then the man thought of something. He held his hand up

to his ear and made it look like a telephone. *"Policía?"* the man asked. *"Teléfono...policía?"*

Then it clicked for Lionel. He had read something in the paper about this. There had been several landings lately. Now that they had made it to dry land, the police could come and get them and run them up to Miami for processing. They'd get their papers and a dishwashing job somewhere, and in maybe a year they'd get their citizenship. "Ahh," Lionel said. "You want me to call the police, right? *Policía?"*

"Sí!" said the man. *"Sí! Teléfono...policía...por favor!"* He enunciated each word slowly so that Lionel could understand.

"All right," said Lionel. "You wait right here, ok?" he motioned for them to remain. "You boys stay right here, all right?" He still had the rod in his hand. "Here," he said to the leader, "you hold onto this. I'll be right back, all right?"

The man nodded and took the rod from him.

"Stay here," repeated Lionel. "You boys don't move, ok? I'll go give 'em a ring, and you guys just stay right here."

All the men nodded and said *"Sí!"* emphatically.

He went up and into the house. He positioned himself so that he could see the group of men out the window in the moonlight. They all stood there in a circle, talking amongst themselves, congratulating themselves and patting each other on the back.

"Yeah," said Lionel once he got an answer on the phone. "Yeah...hey," he said, "it's not an emergency, but I've got half a dozen Cubans just landed in my backyard. Can you send someone over here to wrangle 'em up and take 'em up to Miami?" he gave her the address. "Thank you, ma'am," he said. "Yeah, six of 'em." He counted them again out there on the beach. "Six…uh huh…uh huh…ok, thank you much." He moved to hang up the phone, but then he pulled it back. "And hey," he was able to catch her before she hung up the line, "can you make sure they don't blare their sirens or anything? Don't need to wake up everyone here, you know. Is that all right? Uh huh…uh huh…and can you tell those boys to come right around back? Don't ring the doorbell or anything…yeah…yeah, we'll be right around back by the water, in the back of the house, ok? Uh huh…thank you much, ma'am. You have a good night. Uh huh…thank you much." He hung up the phone.

He looked out the window and saw that the Cubans were still there. Three were standing, and three were sitting down on his log. He headed back out toward the door, and as he did so he reached into the fridge for some beers and went outside. When he got down there, the three on the log stood up when they saw him coming. Then they all stood before him with their arms up again chest-high in front of them.

"No, it's all right, gents," he said. "Sit down, sit down." He motioned for them to sit down again. "Here, boys, have a beer." He reached forward with the open twelve-pack case of beer he'd grabbed from the fridge and handed the cans around. He also handed around a few dish towels so that they could dry themselves off.

"Gracias!" said all the men in turn with little bows of their heads. *"Gracias, señor!"*

They all popped open their beers and took big sips.

"Not much food in the house," said Lionel. "I hope you boys don't mind."

They did not understand, but they just smiled and nodded and sipped their beers. Lionel reached out and took the rod back from the leader and set it down on the log next to him.

"Where you boys from?" he asked.

They didn't seem to understand.

"Cuba?" he asked them.

"Sí! Sí!" said the leader. *"Cuba. Cuba."*

"All right. Cool."

"Sí, Cuba," said the man. *"La Habana."*

"Habana?" said Lionel. "Havana?"

"Sí, Habana," said the man. It was only the leader who spoke, but the other men nodded.

"Funny you all got through," Lionel said, "on account of the full moon and how bright out it is." He motioned up to the sky.

Again, the men did not understand. But they smiled and nodded politely and took another sip of their beers.

They sat in silence for another few minutes, nodding and sipping their beers. Then Lionel heard the doors of two patrol cars slam in the driveway.

"Looks like your ride's here, boys," he said. "Better finish those beers."

He raised his can to the men and took a good sip. They all finished their beers with a laugh.

Four policemen came around the house and came up to them. They had their hands on their pistols, but when they saw Lionel and the men standing around with beers in their hands, they put their weapons away. The six Cuban men all set their cans and towels down next to the log and raised their hands up high above their heads.

"Which one of you called?" asked the first cop.

Lionel raised his hand. "I did, officer. I'm an American."

The man nodded. "These our *Cubanos*?" He gestured to the men with their hands up.

"Sure are," said Lionel.

The four cops lined up the men and started putting them in handcuffs, and then they patted them down in turn. Only one of the cops stood back with his hand on his pistol, just in case, but there was no trouble. The Cuban men stood in a line. The cops used the towels to dry their hands off when they were all through.

"Thank you for the call, sir," the lead cop said. "The Coast Guard just caught another boat out there up near Cudjoe Bay. Couldn't get to shore soon enough, so they'll be sent back. But it looks like these gentlemen made it to shore just fine. Might be more boats coming in tonight, they say."

"That means that these gentlemen get to stay in this country then, doesn't it?" asked Lionel. "Since they got to shore?"

"Guess so," said the cop. "Dry feet. That's the rule. But we just tag 'em and send 'em up to Miami for processing."

The other three cops started leading the men back to the patrol cars. A few of the men called out *"Gracias, señor!"* back to Lionel as they were led away. Then the lead cop took Lionel's name and information and then thanked him and walked back to the car in the driveway. Lionel walked around the house and watched as the men rolled away. He waved to the cars. He wasn't sure if he were waving to the cops or to the Cubans.

Lionel walked back down to the log and picked up his rod. He reeled the line in and didn't feel any pressure, and when the hook came up out of the water he saw that the greenback had worked his way off the hook. He set the hook back onto the reel and tightened the line down. Then he set the rod on the log and picked up his beer and took the last warm sip and looked out toward the water and the moon shining down on it.

"Damn lucky they made it," he said. "Pretty damn lucky, those guys."

A few minutes later, he went back up to the house and opened the screen door. Inside the bedroom he maneuvered in the darkness without turning on the light. The light coming in from the moon outside was good enough to see by. When he reached the bed, Mariah rolled over with a groan.

"You all right?" she asked him.

"Yeah," said Lionel, "I'm fine. Just couldn't sleep, so I went out and threw a line in the water, that's all."

"All right," said Mariah, rolling back. "D'you catch anything?"

"Nah, not a whole lot," said Lionel. "Just a little snapper. It wasn't too big, and I just threw it back. Wasn't worth keeping."

"Uh huh," Mariah grumbled, half asleep. "Ok. Good night then," she said.

Lionel got in bed and set his head on the pillow and closed his eyes. He didn't feel the heartburn too bad, and he thought he might be able to sleep a few hours. "Uh huh, good night," he said. Then he rolled over onto his side and tried to fall asleep.

THE MORNING E TRAIN

You should join a cult. You like wearing white, don't you? Yeah, you like wearing white. You've got those white linen pants from that party that one time, and all those white shirts. Even those dumb white flip-flops Emily got you in Miami. You could be in a cult. No job. No distractions. You could just work in the garden all day. Out in the sun. That's all you wanted—to be out in the sun, right? You could read books and listen to music. Play the guitar. Learn to play the guitar. No, wait, that's not a cult. That's a commune. That's what you meant. A commune. You should join a commune.

No, they'd still come after you. The Feds are always watching those communes. Because they don't believe in paying taxes. The Feds would have their eyes on you right from the start. And then they'd come after you for the tax money anyway. And you can't just leave the country, because they'd eventually find you at some border somewhere. You've thought this all through before.

Then why do you always picture yourself in white? Oh, yeah. Miami. Emily. You always wanted to be on a boat. But not just for a god damn two-hour sunset cruise. You wanted to live on a big yacht, isn't that right? You'd have a pretty blonde wife and nice blonde kids, and even a blonde young nanny. And you'd all be wearing white. That's the way they always look in those sailboat magazines. That's what you really wanted to do, wasn't it? You wanted to be on a sailboat and you wanted to be rich and you wanted to travel the world on your yacht. Yeah, that's what you wanted. How the hell did you forget that?

God, how old are you anyway? Why are you looking at your watch? That's not going to help you. What day is it? Tuesday? Thursday? It was gray outside when you left. What year is it? It's almost your birthday again. Thirty-six this year? Thirty-seven? Weren't you just seventeen? Where the hell did all that go?

The train's made two more stops and you didn't even notice. Or was it three? Or just one? But those two guys are still sitting up there talking. Talking talking talking. What the hell are they talking about, anyway? What the hell's so important? Why do they think everyone wants to hear whatever the hell it is they're talking about? Talk talk

talk. Everyone's talking. Always talking. Everyone's talking about something. Got something they've got to talk about. Is anyone actually saying anything? What the hell is there to say, anyway? It's all been said. Why don't we all just keep our god damn mouths shut? You know, you should keep your mouth shut a bit more often, too. Mouth only gets you into trouble these days. You've never said anything worth a damn in your whole life.

There's someone on your left now. Didn't even notice him sit down. Smells like garbage, and he's sitting too close. Dirty son of a bitch. Bet he'd love to trade places with a suit like you. Bet he thinks you're living in your paradise penthouse. Just riding the subway because you wanted to give the limo driver the day off. Man, you'd give anything to trade places with him right now. Nothing to lose. No one to answer to. No mortgage, no taxes, no bills, no child support. No one even knows his name. Give him your suit and let him walk right into the office. Think they'd even notice? You should trade with him—take that raggedy jacket of his and just start walking. Anywhere. Just start walking and keep on going. Maybe out west. Maybe down south. But anywhere away from here.

God, he smells. Yeah, of course you move away, but he just settles into that inch you just gave him. Right against your arm and leg, too. Just give up. You'll smell like garbage all day. Who cares? This whole god damn city smells like garbage. It's so burned into your nostrils you can't even smell it anymore.

Those two guys up front are still talking. What the hell are they talking about? No one else wants to hear it.

But everyone's just quiet and thinking about being anyplace but here. Look at them all staring—staring down at their phones. Staring straight ahead into the distance. They only move when the train jolts left or right. They all look so gray. Everything is so damn gray. Their faces look like wax. Are they even alive? Hell, you're just another one of them, you know. And you know you're just as dead as they are.

Look at that Asian lady with the surgical mask on. What the hell is she afraid of catching?

Jesus.

Another stop. Yours? Who cares. No, two more. What time is it? Look at your watch. Who cares, you'll get there. Early, late? Late. It doesn't matter.

What the hell happened? Where the hell are you? It wasn't supposed to turn out this way. Miami. That boat. That big white sailboat and those smiling blonde kids. That was what it was supposed to be. What happened to that guy? He was so alive, the way you always pictured him. Where the hell are you now? Just a lump of cold, dead, gray wax like all of the rest of them. And what have you got to show for it? Nothing. What the hell happened to you?

This is your stop. But you want to stay on and keep riding. You don't want to go up into that big gray building anymore. No, you want to get off at some stop further on. Who knows. And you want to get out and start walking.

Maybe west. Maybe south. And you don't want to stop walking until you're somewhere else. Somewhere where you're on a sailboat in white clothes. And yeah, even those damn white flip-flops she bought you. Someplace where all you can see is the god damn bluest ocean you've ever seen all around you, and not another soul for a thousand miles. And the sun so bright it hurts your eyes, but you can't help but laugh from the way it feels on your face. And if it were any better than that you'd burst apart. No, you don't want to get off at this stop. This isn't the stop you want.

But you know what? You're too god damn chicken, aren't you. You're already off the train and out the turnstile and out into the gray street below the gray sky. That big gray building's right in front of you, and there's nothing you can do to keep your legs from taking you in there.

No, you're too god damn chicken.

What the hell happened?

315-B CEDAR AVENUE

B rad woke up at five in the morning to the sound of the engine starting and tires crunching over a fresh layer of snow as the car in the driveway pulled out into the street. He knew that his mother was leaving for good, and he knew why. The only thing he wondered was why she hadn't left sooner.

He looked over in the darkness of the room to see if his brother was awake, but no sounds came from that direction, so he rolled over and tried to go back to sleep. Missing sleep wouldn't help them any.

At six thirty when his alarm went off he went out and saw that the couch where she slept was empty, and even the blankets and pillow were gone. He checked the kitchen table, expecting that maybe she'd left a note or something. But all he found there were the familiar cigarette burns in the checkered tablecloth and the overflowing clay ashtray that he'd made for her in second grade. There was no note on the door, either. It wouldn't have done any good anyway, he thought. There was no doubt she'd taken the car and was on her way to Los Angeles. She had talked a lot about L.A. recently, as if it were Heaven or something. She knew there was a better life for her there. She never said anything to Brad or Nathan, but they'd overhead her sometimes and had pieced it all together.

Brad knew they wouldn't go after her. Lindsay, their mother, knew that, too. No way a sixteen and a twelve year-old were going to travel twelve hundred miles to try and track her down. Nor would they call the police. No, there was nothing left for Brad to do but try to make the best of it. He'd known this was coming for some time now. He knew she'd be leaving them one day or another.

Just before seven o'clock, Nathan woke up and came out to the kitchen.

"Mom left," said Brad.

Nathan poured out his cereal into the bowl and didn't say anything.

"I told you she'd leave us one day, didn't I?" Brad asked. "I told you."

"Uh huh."

"And now she's gone."

Brad looked at his brother and watched him as he poured the milk. He knew Nathan would cry when he was alone, but he wouldn't do it in front of him. Nathan would try to be grown up. But he wasn't yet.

"Pour me a bowl," said Brad.

Nathan got down another bowl and poured out the cereal and milk. He got out two spoons from the drawer and pushed one of the bowls across to Brad.

"Thanks."

"Uh huh."

They ate their cereal in silence.

"You gonna go to school today?" asked Nathan after they had finished.

"Nah," said Brad. "Now that she's gone, I'm not going to school anymore."

"Me either, then," said Nathan.

"No," said Brad, "I'm sixteen, and the law says you have to stay in school until your sixteenth birthday. And now that I'm sixteen, I can get a job without a parent's note. So that's what I'm gonna go do today."

Nathan looked down at the table. Brad knew that Nathan hated school as much as he did.

"As long as I can keep enough money coming in to pay the rent and buy food," said Brad, "then we can get by just fine on our own. Mom never had a plan for us. We didn't fit into her plans. We've gotta make it on our own, all right?"

"Well," said Nathan, "I can get a job, too, then."

"Nah," said Brad. "You start not showing up for school, and then they come looking for us. Just more trouble." He looked at the clock. "You'd better start getting ready for the bus."

Nathan got up from the table and rinsed out his bowl at the sink, and then he went to the bathroom to get ready.

Brad rinsed his bowl and sat back down at the table. Over on the other side was a blank note pad. He reached for it and looked over it. There was some scribbling on it where the pen had pressed through the sheet above and had left little lines and indentations. He couldn't make any of it out as he shifted it in the light. It was a shopping list or something. He took the top page off and ripped it up in little tiny pieces and started making a small pile there in front of him. Then he took the pieces of paper back one by one and ripped them into even smaller pieces until he couldn't rip them anymore. When he was done, he raked the pile of bits into his hand and walked them over to the trash where he watched them fall like confetti into the bin.

Nathan came back out of the bathroom, still in his pajamas.

"I'm not gonna go to school," he said. "I'm gonna get a job, too. Shoveling snow or something."

Brad shook his head. "Look," he said, "you're gonna go to school. Either that or they come looking for us, all right? And besides, you're too young to work. No one would give a twelve year-old a job, you got that?"

Nathan looked down at the floor.

"You got that?" Brad repeated.

"Uh huh," he mumbled.

"Now, you go on and get ready for school," said Brad.

Nathan turned back around and went to get dressed.

Around seven thirty, Nathan came out of the room and walked to the door with his backpack on. Brad came up to him.

"Now, you don't say nothing to nobody about this," he said. "If they find out it's just you and me and no parents here, they'll send us to Social Services, and we'll end up in a home somewhere. Probably split us up."

Nathan nodded but didn't say anything.

"You don't want that, do you?"

Nathan shook his head that he understood.

"You and me, we can do just fine on our own. You understand? Mom or no mom. Don't tell nobody, okay?"

Nathan nodded his head silently. He understood. But he knew that if he tried to speak, he would cry. If he could just get out the door without speaking, he'd be fine and he wouldn't cry in front of Brad.

"Okay," said Brad, "you have a good day at school and you do all right in your classes. You make good grades, and don't get into any trouble. That's all you can do right now, okay?"

Nathan shook his head again, and the two boys gave each other a quick but awkward hug. Nathan went out the door to walk to the bus stop, and Brad shut the door behind him.

Brad went back to the kitchen and got a pencil from the counter. He sat down with the pad of paper and started writing notes. He knew he needed a plan—it was all there in his mind, but now he needed to get it down. Rent, job, and food were the first items he wrote down. Then he made a list of places he would go to apply for jobs. He was sixteen, and he knew there was no reason to stay in school any longer. He wasn't meant to go to college or do anything important with his life other than work for a paycheck, so there was no reason to put it off. All the jobs he could get right now didn't require a diploma. And anyways, he could get his GED if he needed it, and that would be just fine. He scribbled down the list and marked off the places he would go today. There were all the burger joints and all the gas stations and tire shops. That would be a start. And at minimum wage, that would just about pay the rent. But there were also the junkyard, the car parts store, and the Food-Mart, where at least he could get a job moving boxes or stocking shelves. If he got to be a bagger, there would be tips. And he was pretty good at changing tires and washing windshields, and he knew enough about cars to work at the auto parts store.

He skipped down a few lines. Today was the nineteenth, and he knew that Lindsay had left no money behind for them. He had eleven days to scrape together six hundred bucks. He walked around the house and looked at all things that he could sell. They could probably get a hundred or two for all the furniture and appliances they wouldn't need. He could sell the sofa, tables and chairs, the beds, and the dressers. They could keep all the blankets and mattress covers and use those to sleep on the floor. There was no TV, but he could try to get a few bucks for the lamps and the blender and the toaster. He also had a few bucks saved up, but it probably wasn't more than about thirty or forty dollars. But he had some friends and could call in a few favors. Maybe even get a few bucks here and there on loan. It might be just enough to get by, just until he had his first paycheck or two. So as he looked over his list, he nodded his head and had a good enough feeling they'd do just fine after the first month. The biggest thing he needed to do was to make rent on the first. Then there'd be the electricity, gas, and water.

He went around to all the cupboards and made a mental inventory. There was enough food to last them about two weeks, as long as they weren't picky. Cereal boxes and canned food and a few things in the freezer, but not much in the fridge. They'd eat a lot of instant pancakes and canned peas. That was enough to get by on. He'd only have to buy milk here and there. And he knew bread and bananas were pretty cheap. He checked the bathroom and saw that they were down to three rolls of toilet paper. You could get that for free most places you went, if you tore off as much as you could and stuffed it in your pockets, or you could fit a whole roll under your jacket. He'd have Nathan try to bring some back from school each day in his backpack.

He looked at the clock. It was almost eight. He got on the phone.

"Jimmy," he said when there was an answer. "Yeah, hey, I'm gonna sell you that stack of nudie mags you wanted. Yeah. Thirty bucks, like I said. Yeah, thirty. Okay." He hung up the phone.

He dialed again.

"Josh," he said. "Yeah, hey, it's Brad. How much would you give me for that fishing reel of mine? The green one. Yeah, I know everything's iced over. Ten bucks? Make it twenty. No? All right, never mind." He hung up the phone and thought about who he could call next.

After the phone, he went back and finished out his list of jobs he would apply for, and he scratched out a few he knew wouldn't take him at sixteen, like the auto parts store. Then he went to take a shower, shaved the stubble on his lip and chin, and put on some decent clothes. He needed a haircut, but he'd have to go without for now.

As Brad stepped out into the cold and locked the door behind him, he thought about Lindsay and her situation. He couldn't blame his mother for what she'd done. She'd gotten pregnant at fifteen and had him when she was just sixteen years old. Brad was sixteen now, so Lindsay had given up an entire half of her life to raise him and Nathan. Two fathers that they had never known, and just a bunch of loser boyfriends here and there. Maybe she was on her way to L.A. with one of them. He knew he couldn't blame her for leaving. Hell, she might really be able to find a better life out there, one way or another. She sure wasn't getting anywhere with him and Nathan holding her down. All she wanted was her life back, and he could understand that. Still, he thought, it was a pretty raw thing to do. He stepped out into the snow and walked around to the back of the duplex. Hell, thought Brad, if Lindsay had to grow up at sixteen, maybe he would have to grow up a little bit, too. He would have to do it someday, so why not now?

He brushed the snow off his bike and unlocked the chain. He set out down the driveway and onto Cedar Avenue where the plows had already been and had salted the streets. He pumped a few times and got the bike moving. He pictured the list that was in his pocket in his mind, and he hoped he could get a job just a few blocks away. Hank's BBQ was the closest place on the list. He'd wash dishes or bus tables. He'd sweep and mop and flip burgers or man the smoker out back. Maybe they could get some of the leftover food each night. He pumped a few more times and got up to speed, then shifted up a gear and settled into a nice cruising speed through the slush and the cold wind. He looked down at the bike and thought about who he knew who might want it. He could probably get thirty or forty bucks for it and then buy it back a few weeks later if he needed it. It was all on him now, just as he'd known it would be one day. He had Nathan to worry about now, and he wouldn't just give in like Lindsay had. No, he thought as he pumped the pedals harder against a coming hill, he'd give it the best he had.

CHARTER BOAT ROW

Evan got tired of waiting in the ninety-degree afternoon sun and locked up the boat and headed across the street to Percy's bar. He sat there smoking a cigarette at a worn, gray picnic table outside for several minutes before the waitress saw him and came out.

"Yeah," said Evan, "let me take a swim in that bottle of rum I like so much. You know the one."

The waitress nodded without speaking and tucked away her pen and paper into her server belt and walked back inside. Evan wondered why she ever came out with her pen and paper when she saw him. She'd been working there six or seven weeks now, and he never ordered food or anything—nothing more than a drink. She should know that by now. Hell, he thought, they should be on a first name basis. He lit up another of his cheap hand-rolled cigarettes that he had spent the afternoon rolling on board, and he realized he'd never even looked at her nametag. The waitress brought the glass out and set the bottle on the table.

"I brought the bottle," she said. "There was only a little bit left. I'm sure you'll finish it."

Evan looked at it and knew that he would. He thanked her and poured himself a sip.

"Damn!" he said aloud after she'd left. He had forgotten to catch her nametag again.

He was well into his second glass there under the bright banana-yellow umbrella when Ken, the captain of the *Miss Sizzle*, two boats down, showed up.

"No bites today?" asked Evan.

Ken sat down at the table and picked up the bottle of rum and rolled it back and forth in his hands. He set the bottle back down. The waitress had seen him coming and brought another glass and set it on the table.

"Nope, no bites," he said when she had gone. "No one wants to go fishing these days. Maybe it's too damn hot out."

"Yeah," said Evan. "Pretty hot."

"The fishing's good enough," continued Ken, "but no one wants to go out. We're missing all those sails out there, and all the kings. Kings are running all right this last week or so. Nah, they all want to go on those big party boats and toss frozen squid down to the grunts and get their lines all tangled up for fifty bucks. But they're missing all the really good fishing."

"Uh huh," said Evan.

"Anyone else get out today?" asked Ken.

"Nah," said Evan. "Tommy took someone out the other day, and they hooked up on three sails. Didn't bring any in, though. They brought back a king or two, and some amberjack, and a cooler full of bonito."

"Yeah," said Ken. "Tommy told me that. I haven't had a trip out in a week. We're missing all the good fishing, and this is supposed to be the high season. Lots of people down here, but no one wants to go out."

"Well, what the hell are they all down here for then?" asked Evan.

"Boozin', I guess," said Ken.

"Yeah. Boozin', I guess."

They each took a sip from their glasses and tasted the rum. It was a good, dark rum that took a sip or two to get used to in the heat. But it felt good once it was down.

"Hey," said Evan, "where's Mandy? Haven't seen her around these last few days."

"Yeah," said Ken. He was silent for a few moments. "She left."

"Left, huh?" said Evan. He was swirling his glass around on the table out of boredom.

"Yeah, she left. Two days ago. Told me she was going."

Evan considered this for a moment. "Left, like she went to get cigarettes?" he asked, making a joke at Ken's expense. "Or left left?"

"Yeah, she left left." Ken wasn't laughing.

"Hmm," said Evan more seriously. "She coming back, you think?"

"Who knows," said Ken. "She's left before, ya know, but she always came back next day. But then she didn't come back yesterday, so I think she might've gone for good this time."

"Hmm. Doesn't want to accept her lot in life, then," said Evan. "Not happy with who she is and the hand she's been dealt. That right?"

"Yeah, I guess that's it. She'll fight it until the day she dies, I suppose."

"We ain't got it so bad, though," Evan waved the thought away with his hand in the air. "Water, sun. This is paradise, man. It ain't perfect, but it ain't so bad."

"Agreed," said Ken. "Not sure why she thinks there's such a better life out there somewhere for her. This ain't so bad sittin' here."

Evan laughed to himself. He wiped a drop of sweat off his cheek. "I guess I can't be too upset about that. You know I never really liked her that much. Not like your old girl Natalie. Mandy gets a little uppity sometimes. With me she does, anyway."

"Yeah, I know," said Ken. "She wasn't my favorite either. But she could cook a little, and she was a cheap drunk, so it only took three or four beers to get her in the sack. I guess I kinda liked her enough, anyway. Liked having her around."

"Well, I'm sorry a little then," said Evan. "Where'd she run off to this time?"

"Same as last, I guess. Said she didn't want to be down here in the Keys anymore. Guess she caught a one-way bus ticket to Miami. But after that, who knows. New York or L.A. Take your pick."

Evan pulled away his shirt that was sticking to his chest. He waved it back and forth to let some cool air in. There was no breeze out there, and no fans. The fans were inside, but they only pushed the hot air around. "Still thinks she can make it as a singer then?" he said.

"Yeah. Don't know how she plans to make it at forty-two, but she thinks she's got something. Thinks she's meant for something more than cutting bait and slinging beers to tourists. Like I said, New York or L.A. Only places you can go for that sort of business."

"Sure, sure."

The waitress came back out to see if there were any new tables filled, but there weren't any. She started to go back in.

"Miss? Can you bring me a beer please?" asked Ken with a wave of his hand.

The waitress stopped and looked back from the door. "Sure," she said, "what kind you want?"

"Anything cold, honey," said Ken. "Nothing light." He finished the sip of rum and pushed the glass away with a flick of his fingers. "Need something cold for the heat. Need a beer."

"Well," said Evan, "you don't have to convince me. I just like this bottle I found on the shelf in there the other day. Nearly cleaned the whole thing off by now." He picked up the bottle and rolled it in his hands and looked at the label as Ken had done. "Guatemala," he said. "Decent stuff. Three or four glasses, and I'm feelin' pretty good."

Both of the men sat in silence and stared out at the boats along the docks. The marina was filled with a whole fleet of charter boats, but most of the captains had already lost hope for the day and had locked up or were scrubbing down again. The big party boats had gone out, of course, but only one charter boat had gone out that morning. They kept watching. A family was walking along the docks and reading the various signs with the names of the boats, the captains, and what they went after. No one boat was different from any other, really. The family stopped in front of the *Renegade II*, Evan's boat.

"Looks like you've got a bite," said Ken. "You wanna go reel 'em in?"

Evan looked at his glass of rum and took a sip. "Nah," he said, "you can go try if you want to."

"All right," said Ken. "Wish me luck."

Evan grunted. That was good enough for luck.

Ken was gone for ten minutes talking to them and came back and sat down. He took a sip of his warm beer that was sitting there.

"You hook 'em?" asked Evan finally.

"Yeah," said Ken. "I think so. Said they'd come by tomorrow afternoon. I tried to get them there in the morning. Said the fishing was way better in the morning, which it is. But they said they wanted to come back in the afternoon. Just the guy and his son, not the wife and the girl. Would've been nice to have the wife on board. Something to look at anyway. The girl was a bit too young to look at. Not for me, but in general."

Evan poured a small sip of rum in his glass and swirled it around. "You think they'll show, then?"

"Who knows," said Ken. "Not many do. But I'll take a trip if I can get it."

"Should've gotten fifty bucks out of him, anyway," said Evan. "Make him commit. At least then if they didn't show you'd have the fifty bucks."

"Yeah," said Ken. "I knew I should've, but I didn't. Who knows, they might show tomorrow. Maybe they'll show."

"Yeah, maybe."

They sat there and sipped on their drinks for a while, not speaking.

"What you got your boys doing?" asked Evan.

"Not too many trips lately," said Ken, "so I told 'em I couldn't pay 'em. Told 'em I'd give 'em a call if we got anything. I'll give 'em a call tonight and see if they'd be available tomorrow. Guess I only need one. But then I'll call 'em in the morning if I feel good enough about it, because I don't want them showing up when there's no work. Then I've still got to pay 'em."

"Yep."

"They've got other jobs, you know. In town. Only so much scrubbing you can do on a boat at the dock when there's no fishing to be done."

"Sure," said Evan. "My boat's cleaner than it's ever been. Couldn't get any shinier."

Ken wiped his dark brown neck of sweat. The beer was no relief from the heat. "If this goes on another season or two, I might have to consider selling the boat. Or at least taking out another loan on it."

"Yeah," said Evan. "Me, too. It's been that way for going on three years now. Can't get ahead any single season."

Ken swirled his beer around in the bottle. "Maybe it's about time I got another job, too," he said. "This charter business sure isn't paying right now."

"Yeah, I know that," said Evan. "What else you gonna do?"

"Nothing else I'm good at," said Ken. "Pretty good at fishing. And driving a boat. Maybe I can get a job driving one of them ferries out to the Tortugas or up to Fort Myers. Or maybe one of them dolphin sightseeing boats. Steady paycheck, anyway."

The waitress came out and brought another beer for Ken.

"Got a deal for you," said Ken when she had left.

"Shoot."

"You get my beers this afternoon, and I won't call my boys for tomorrow."

"Uh huh."

"I'll let you be mate tomorrow on the boat, if we take that guy and his boy out."

Evan thought for a moment and nodded.

"No pay, of course," said Ken, "but you'll probably get a decent tip out of it. More than the beers, anyways. Better than nothing."

Evan nodded. "Yeah, sure. That sounds all right."

They sat there for another few minutes, and Ken had his beer. Evan was nearly to the bottom of the bottle of rum. He lit up another cigarette and offered one to Ken, but he didn't want one. They both stared out at the boats through their dark, polarized sunglasses. Then they saw someone they recognized. She was walking over by the *Miss Sizzle*. They both knew her right away.

"Well," said Evan. "Look who's back."

Ken didn't say anything, but he was watching her as well. She had both her suitcases with her, one in each hand. Everything she owned was in those suitcases.

"Looks like she got to Miami and turned right back around," said Evan.

"Who knows," said Ken. "Who knows with that one."

"Well," asked Evan, "you gonna go over there?"

Ken sat back in his chair. "No, not yet. Maybe I should just let her get settled back in first. Not scare her off."

"Yeah, maybe."

Mandy went on board, and they didn't see her for a few minutes. Then she came back out on deck and off the boat onto the dock and walked right over to Percy's. She walked over to their table and sat right down right next to Ken. No one said anything. The waitress came out and walked over.

"Can I get you a drink, ma'am?" she asked.

"Sure, Lori," she said. "I'll have a beer like him."

So, her name was Lori, thought Evan. He repeated it to himself so that he'd remember it. But he knew he'd probably forget.

"All right," said the waitress. "Another one for you, too?" she asked Ken.

He nodded.

The waitress looked at Evan and at the bottle of rum. "We don't have another bottle of that," she said, "but I can bring you another kind, if you want."

"Hmm," said Evan, "Then I'll have a beer like them, too, Lori." It was too damn hot for rum, anyway.

"All right," said the waitress. "Three beers." The waitress brought the bottles back out and set them down.

They all took a sip. No one said anything to Mandy, and she didn't say anything back until their beers were nearly gone. Finally, she did speak.

"You got any jobs coming up?" she asked.

"Yeah," said Ken. "Tomorrow afternoon. Just two guys—a dad and his son. Evan's gonna come out with me and be mate."

Mandy nodded. "All right," she said. "You think they're gonna show?"

Ken nodded. "Yeah," he said, "I think so."

"You get any money from them?"

"Nah," said Ken. "But I think they'll show."

They all sipped their beers for a few minutes until a new round came out.

"So," said Ken, "you back then?" He hadn't wanted to say it, but it came out on its own.

"Yeah," said Mandy. "I'm back."

Ken nodded. He wasn't going to ask anything more—there was no reason to.

Then, when Mandy looked away, he nodded to Evan, and Evan nodded back. They both understood. She was back, all right. She was back until something better came along. And Ken was all right with that, and sometimes that's the best you can get. They both knew that there was something to be said for knowing your lot in life, for knowing that good is good enough. Mandy didn't know that yet, and she never would. She'd fight that forever, no matter how good she ever had it. But Evan and Ken knew that, and they knew that this was pretty damn close to paradise. And they knew that it would never get much better than this. And that was good enough for them.

DIXIE'S LAST RUN

"You know this is it, don't you, girl?" Brandon said to Dixie as he took off her collar and laid it up on the table. "Last one." He stood up and looked out the window. The sun had nearly set. Dusk was approaching, and soon it would be time to go.

Even though her eyes showed she understood, Dixie wagged her head and tail slowly as she did every time they were getting ready to go out. She knew what having her collar off meant. She could get closer up on the birds that much easier without the jingle of her tags against the metal clasp. She wagged her tail so hard that a solid stream of urine splashed on the ground without her knowing.

Brandon saw it. It had been happening a lot lately. Her hips had just about given out.

"That's all right, girl," he said as he pulled off some paper towel, wetted it under the sink, and wiped up the wood floor. "You didn't even feel that, did you?"

Behind him, the two young bird dog pups that had finished their training and had already been on four successful hunts with him whined and yelped in their large metal cage. He had baited them in with treats and had locked them in there a few minutes before. But now they could see that Brandon was going out for a hunt and wondered why he was leaving them in the cage. They whined and clawed the bars, pacing back and forth, barking loudly. This was what they lived for, this was all they wanted—to be out in the air and the grass, and free to chase after the birds in the fields. They craved the hunt.

Dixie felt proud that she was going out with Brandon. She had been his only dog for so many years. But the arrival of the two new rambunctious English Pointer pups a month ago had made her uneasy, and so she was glad to be going out with Brandon alone. The last several times they had all gone out, she had not been able to keep up with them at all. The Pointers had sent up the birds too soon, and Brandon had been too far back to get the shot he wanted. They needed to learn some patience.

"You're all right with this, then?" Brandon asked her as he stroked the top of her head. He looked into her deep black eyes, and she looked back into his. Brandon nodded.

She definitely seemed to understand, he thought, and he could sense she was fine with it. The pain was getting to her more and more. He couldn't stand to watch her walk around the house each day. She moaned in her sleep most nights, and he'd had to help her up the stairs from the yard these last few weeks. She couldn't even bark with much force anymore because it set off a pain in her abdomen that made her whine. They both knew it was time for her to go.

Brandon reached up to grab his pump-action Remington 12-gauge, but as he pulled the shells out of the box he decided instead that a rifle would be better. The rifle would make less of a mess, he thought. Even at close range the shotgun could be messy. When he had thought this all through last week, he hadn't thought of that. He put everything back up and stared at the rack and thought for a minute. Then he pulled down the Winchester Model 70 bolt action with the .308 bore. He stood the rifle on the ground against the wall and filled the bullet band and fixed it to the butt. As he did so, he could feel Dixie standing there with her shoulder against his leg, breathing hard.

With the two Pointer pups in their cage yelping and pacing, he opened the door, and Dixie led him outside, slowly making her way down the steps. When she made it to the ground he had to help her back up to her feet. A few yards from the door they passed Brandon's aluminum canoe up on its rack. Dixie had always been great in the canoe, he thought. She sat perfectly still and wouldn't make a sound, even when she saw the ducks not a few yards away. She had always been great no matter what they were hunting. Best Boykin Spaniel he'd ever known, and certainly the best flusher he'd ever seen. With her long, dark brown curls she could hide in any brush and allow Brandon to get right up on the birds before she sent them up. And she knew the perfect moment to do it. He'd always had a good shot with her.

The sun had set now, and they started out down the trail with Dixie leading the way. She stayed only a few feet ahead of him the best she could, and Brandon walked slow enough so that she could stay out ahead of him. She moved very slowly now. He watched her long dark curls on her ears bouncing sluggishly. He watched as every dozen steps or so her hips would give out and she would lose a step and catch herself with a look back at him, and then continue on.

It was a quarter of a mile from the house before they broke the tree line and the field opened up and stretched all the way around for several miles over the flat ground. This was the best hunting ground around, and they were lucky that it was so close. This was where Dixie had spent the best years of her life; and Brandon, too, for that matter. This was where he had first taken her out as a little pup to train her when his father had given her to him for Christmas at eleven. That was sixteen years ago now, he thought. It seemed like a week. He thought about this and knew he should have put her down sooner. He had let it go on too long, and she had gotten really bad. He knew he should have done something for her much sooner.

They got off the trail and went into the tall grass. Dixie started sniffing to see if she could pick something up. Her sense of smell had nearly left her, but she concentrated the best she could. She smelled the moist grass and the dirt, but there was little else there. She gave a look back to Brandon. He nodded to her encouragingly.

Brandon walked forward and led her the way he knew he had to go, then let her back in front. She looked back at him now and then, and from where he was walking she judged where he wanted to go and tried her best to stay out in front of him. She knew she was not really leading the way, but she was doing her best. She didn't want to let Brandon down.

All of a sudden, Brandon whispered to her. "What do you smell, girl?" he said. "You see somethin'?"

Dixie hadn't smelled anything, but she heard his voice and had heard the click of the safety of the rifle coming off. She started to wag her tail. Brandon looked up and heard some birds making their way through the grass in the distance. Could have been crows, or doves, or maybe quail. Dixie didn't hear anything. Her ears were bad, and her eyes were cloudy from the cataracts.

He spoke to her again. "What do you see, girl?" he asked her.

She was getting more excited. Even though she couldn't see or hear anything, she could sense Brandon was onto something. He was right behind her. She grew tense, and her tail stopped moving. She was trying to pick up any sound she could. She looked back at him for only a moment to see where he was and saw that he was just a step behind her, and then she looked ahead and tried to focus in the dim light. She knew it was her job to spring ahead and send the birds up for him. She didn't know where they were, but she would do her best.

"I see somethin' up ahead, Dixie!" Brandon whispered intensely. "You ready, girl? You ready?"

Dixie's heart was pounding. This was her moment. She grew tense and eager. Her senses were peaked, and she prepared her body to leap forward and to scare up whatever lay ahead. Any pain in her hips was gone now. She was too thrilled to feel any pain.

Brandon raised up the barrel of the rifle and drew the muzzle to the base of her head. He blinked once or twice and aimed the best he could. He knew that he couldn't shake or it would make it bad for her. He spoke to her one last time.

"Go, Dixie!" he whispered as quickly and intensely as he could. "Go get 'em!"

With all the energy Dixie had left inside of her she threw everything back into her hind legs to take a leap forward. This was her moment. She was going to give Brandon everything she had. She sprung forward.

An instant later, she fell to the ground.

Brandon did not hear the crack of the rifle itself, but a second later he did hear the echo come back to him from the tree line back by the house. Several quail flew up into the air just a few feet in front of him. He didn't notice them. The sound seemed to echo and reverberate for several minutes as he stood there, resounding within him and all around him.

Brandon's body was frozen. It took him a minute to come back to himself. And when he did, he set the rifle down and sat down next to Dixie with his leg against her warm, lifeless body. For several minutes he did not look at her. But he could sense that it was all over and that the single shot had done the job. He had done a good thing—he had ended it all for her at her brightest moment. That was the best he could do for her.

His father had told him about this day many years ago. Brandon was only fourteen at the time, but his father had pulled him aside and had told him that one day he would have to put Dixie down, when her time had come she couldn't hunt anymore. Brandon had never thought that day would actually come. As a young pup she had so much life in her. He didn't know too much about death back then. Sure, he could kill birds and squirrels and deer and could see the death in all of it. He had a solid respect for death. But it was not the same with the death of something or someone you loved. This was different. And now, the day his father had told him about had finally come. And the moment he had dreaded for so long had come and gone.

"Just make sure you do it right," his father had said to him. "She's a good dog. She'll deserve it. And you'll know what to do."

Brandon knew he had let it get too bad for her. But he also knew that when the time came he had done it right, the best way he knew how. And he hoped his father would be proud of him for the way he had done it.

After several minutes of silence, staring off into the dark blue dusk around him, he looked over at Dixie. He moved around toward her head and looked into her wet, black eyes in the growing darkness. He saw happiness there in her face. Happiness and understanding. Understanding that she'd known what he'd had to do. He had given her that moment she deserved—that moment of absolute joy, of anticipation, of doing a good job for Brandon. He only wished one day that he could have the same. No tears came to his eyes. Just emptiness. Nothing but black emptiness.

It was growing dark. He did not know how long he'd been sitting there, but he knew there was business to get on with. He had planned all this out several days ago. He had come out with a shovel and had dug the hole and had planned how he would do it. Moving away from Dixie's body, he found the handle of the shovel sticking up in the tall grass maybe twenty yards away. He had prepared for everything. There was a sheet there, and he took the folded sheet and took it back to Dixie. He laid it out flat next to her and then pulled her legs up and rolled her over onto it. Then he took one last look at her and threw the rest of the sheet over her body. He grabbed the ends and dragged her over the tall grass toward the grave. When he got there, he grabbed the corners and lifted her down, getting on his hands and knees. The hole was five or six feet deep. He had made it deep enough so that nothing would come and dig her up, not even a bear. He grabbed the shovel and started filling it in and tossed the dirt down over her as softly as he could.

It was twenty minutes later and he patted down the last of the dirt and then stepped on it to smooth it down. It would take a whole season for the grass to grow over, and then he would never know exactly where she was. He didn't leave a marker—she was where she needed to be, and that was all that mattered.

He grabbed up the shovel and the rifle and walked back home in the near darkness. It was getting so that he wasn't able to see well, until he approached the house and he could see the lights he had left on inside.

When he went inside, the two Pointers were yelping, and he let them out of the cage and out the back door so that they could run around and chase each other and wear themselves out. He didn't want to hear them barking, and he wanted to be alone.

He emptied the bullet band back into the box—there had only been the need for the one round. He had thrown the casing far into the grass somewhere when it was over and he had ejected it from the chamber. It was cold in there, so he lit a fire and poured himself a glass of bourbon and sat down in the chair his father used to sit in, before his father had passed and his mother had moved south so that she wouldn't have to shovel anymore snow in the winters. He wished he could speak to his father now and let him know that Dixie was gone, and his father would know that he had done it all right in the end. He sat in the chair and could almost feel the warmth of Dixie there at his feet where she had always been. He could hear his father's voice speaking softly to his mother in the next room.

And as he sat there, hearing the young dogs yelping outside as they ran around in the dark, he thought to himself. They'd be good dogs, he decided. They'd need a few months more training, and above all they needed to learn a little patience. Maybe he would start taking them out one at a time until they got their skills up. They'd never be near as good as Dixie, of course. But, he nodded as he took a slow sip and felt the warmth of the fire, they'd be good dogs. He'd make them into good dogs, all right.

A SPLENDID
WEEK-LONG AFFAIR

The girl sat lazily yet elegantly in the chair, her legs resting on the table and crossed at the knees so that her golden skin shone bright in the afternoon sun. Blue smoke whipped from her lips and around her face in a fragile stream as she charmed it with a look of her eyes and a flick of her wrist. Nick watched her movements and thought how tragic she looked there and how she belonged in this same place but in a different time.

The pastis from the drink in his hand was getting to him now, and he smiled at the way he felt it move through his body and out to his fingers. He had made it strong with only a few cubes of ice and a splash of water that had made the drink turn a yellowish-white. The ice by now had all but melted, but the drink was still cool, and little beads of sweat wandered down the glass and onto the table. The girl had been watching him for a few minutes as he smiled and followed the smoke from her cigarette up to where the air caught it and took it away far above them.

"What makes you smile?" she asked. Her placid voice had broken his isolation.

He lifted his head slowly and looked at her with narrowed eyes, not because of the sun but because he was somewhere else just then.

"The taste of the drink." He answered her simply, and there was only silence as they both thought on these words and then just listened and watched the boats move beneath them in the expansive harbor below.

High on the balcony there it was not windy as it had been across the sea early that morning as he'd stood alone, still awake from the night before to see the sun rise. It was now bright and cool, and the warm, sweet air of the evening had not yet come, though it seemed only moments away.

"I want to go down to the sea," she said, once again breaking the soft stillness that surrounded them. "Will you come with me?"

"I'll just finish my drink," he said, taking another sip.

"Will the water be cold?" she asked.

He did not answer. The mood there was occupied with thoughtful distraction, and Nick caught himself thinking about the party the night before—about the couples and the dancing and the fine smell of perfume and the blur of the colors of young men and women moving in and out among the handsome crowd.

The girl's name was Eva. Nick did not believe that for some reason, but it was what she had called herself when they had met at a dinner party in Cannes a few nights before, surrounded by the voices and the music, together, but apart from it all. All he knew for certain was that she was not American. He'd caught her speaking a few words of French and a few of Spanish and Italian, but the accent was indiscernible. She had been with him three days now at the *Hôtel*. He didn't know where she had come from or where she was headed, and he knew it did not matter. He felt that asking too many questions might ruin this, and this was something he wanted right now. It was something pleasant and frail, and he would not disturb it for fear of losing it.

The girl pulled something from her pocket, and only after a few minutes and a few more sips from his glass did Nick notice that she had been reading.

"Where did you get that?" he asked, half interested, half indifferent, and fully engulfed in the tingle of the aromatic drink on his lips.

"It was next to the bed. On the table. What is it?" she asked. "Is this your writing?" She held up the black little leather-bound book, and Nick laughed.

"Oh, that's nothing."

She held her cigarette loosely between her fingers and turned the pages and felt the rough paper on her skin. Her eyes moved excitedly over the words as if she read them but did not understand them. "I see that. I think it is very good," she said.

"Hardly," muttered Nick. "It's just some notes and things I scribble down as they come into my head."

"Well, I like it very much."

He sat there a minute longer and watched her flip through the pages with a fascinated look as she mouthed the words and he could not tell what she was saying. He wondered if she understood his words and what they really meant.

"Is there anything about me in here? Do you write about me?"

Nick shook his head. "No, I haven't written about you."

"But you want to?"

"Of course." Nick had wondered how he wanted to capture her, if he could. But he knew he would not be able to write about this the way he saw it and the way he felt it just now—the way it needed to be written. At least not yet. He knew all that would come long after.

She read one of the lines to him, but he did not hear her. Something about the mundane things in life being misconstrued as art. "What does that mean?" she asked.

Nick thought for a minute and then remembered the line and when he had written it and repeated it back to himself under his breath. "I was in a strange mood when I wrote that," he said. "Not myself."

She laughed. "It is very depressing. It is very sad to think such things." He knew that was true.

Nick took another sip from his drink and was more aware of her there now, and of the light breeze and the sun and the sounds from the water below. In the distance from where he could not see it, a boat sounded its horn in two long blasts that echoed in the harbor. When the sound faded, it instilled a new, more powerful silence that settled heavily over them. He smiled at her and reached out and ran his hand through the girl's short dark hair and thought of how young she looked there, and she held his hand and pressed it hard against her cheek. He felt her cool skin, and he himself felt warm and pleased there in the sun.

She set the book down softly in her lap and breathed in the smoke from her cigarette and let it pour smoothly from her lips and swirl up and away from her. "I will write something for you in here," she said to him. "I think you will like it."

The summer was slow for the small town of Beaulieu-sur-Mer. Nearly everyone was a few train stops away in Monaco or Nice or Cannes where the attraction of smooth pebble beaches and the occasional film star could not be resisted. But Nick liked the way the coarse sand made him feel and enjoyed his relative solitude here in Beaulieu. He didn't even mind that the trains stopped running here around ten thirty and that he had to either sleep at the parties he attended or catch a ride with a friend or a cab back to his hotel. Most mornings he found himself among the other guests strewn about the sofas and guestrooms from the night before, often four or five fully clothed guests to a bed. But the thought of ending the night at its peak and venturing off into the darkness or into the reality of the world again was not something any of them wanted to bear. And so his '62 Alfa Romeo convertible and its leather interior often sat open to the cool mist that settled along the coast each night.

Across the street from his hotel were a comfortable café and a tobacco store where Nick found himself most afternoons, as well as a clothing boutique next to the café, where Nick and the girl had gone earlier that morning to buy her a bathing suit. It seemed that the only clothes she had with her fit in her oversized purse that Nick had noticed by her side when he'd first met her. But their swimwear venture was a failed one, as the distraction of a bright yellow dress in the window fully occupied the girl.

"I could never have such a dress!" said the girl. "Just look at it! My mother used to have one like it when I was little. I always dreamed of wearing her dress."

Nick liked it too. It made the girl look like an advertising poster for perfume that they had seen at the bus stops in Cannes. The glow of the girl's face decided it for him. Only after they returned to the hotel and she mentioned going to the pool did he realize they had forgotten their reason for going to the store in the first place. She tried the dress on for him in the store when they bought it and again when they arrived back at the hotel after lunch, he supposed to show him how much she really liked it. But then she folded it smartly and placed it back in the cream-colored box it had come in and tied the blue ribbon back on it. So, when she went swimming that afternoon, she borrowed a pair of his shorts and tied them tight around her waist and wore a shirt that he had in is closet that was too small for him to wear any longer. Still, his clothes were much too big on her, and Nick resolved to get her a bathing suit the next time they left the hotel. There was really no one else on the beach near the hotel, except for the occasional group of young children out of school. Around the room she wore a short chambray skirt she'd had with her and a button-down white pajama shirt of Nick's that was far too big on her. There were other clothes she could have worn, but she said she liked the outfit.

The dresses she wore to parties in the evenings she was able to pick out from among the fifteen or so in Nick's closet that had been left by his fiancée Laura who, several weeks prior, had ended their engagement in a very public manner during dinner with a group of friends. Laura had caught the morning train to Marseilles and then to Paris the very next day, and that was the last he had seen of her. He'd heard from friends since then that she had flown to London. "Why London?" Nick had thought. They had never been to London together. He didn't know why, and he wasn't too concerned with the details after buying her the train ticket and seeing her out the door to the waiting cab.

Now this young girl Eva—though Nick never thought of her by her name—simply didn't leave after spending that first night with him after the party, as if she had nowhere else to be; and he, surprising himself, simply didn't ask any questions. When he found her still there the next evening at dinner, he decided he would just as well have her stay another night. And the next day he had the man at the front desk give him an extra key to his room so that she could come and go as she pleased.

Today was a Tuesday, and as the girl was down at the water in a pair of his shorts, Nick sat down to get off three letters he had been putting off for several weeks now. He pulled out a few sheets of paper and three envelopes and sat at the table near the big window facing the sea in the room to write, but not without pouring himself a drink first. He placed the bottle of Ricard next to him after filling his glass halfway with water and ice and pouring the yellow liquid on top. He sat there and, instead of mixing it, he watched the pastis seep down between the pieces of ice and turn his glass white.

It was a long, hot summer this season on the Med, and Nick made sure to mention that to each of his correspondents, along with other pertinent details of his life in the last two months, including the end of his engagement with Laura. He wrote about the friends he had seen so far this season and the friends he had not seen. It was the latter that seemed most important to him. But he did not mention the girl, not even to his brother in New York who would take some pleasure in reading his initial thoughts of her. It wasn't something he needed to write about just now. The other letters went out to a friend of his who was a sculptor whose work he had seen highlighted in a Marseilles newspaper, and to a former business partner of his who was serving three months for hitting a cop during a fight at a baseball game in Philly.

When he was finished, he poured himself another drink and considered walking down to the beach to watch the girl swim. She was a fish, this one. Most days she spent swimming in the sea out as far as she could and back. He was content just to watch her from shore and make the occasional venture out to her as she returned when he got too hot on the sand. But when he swam out to her she didn't come to meet him, but instead kept swimming toward shore as if she hadn't even seen him. He didn't mind. He liked watching her and enjoyed when she finally came back to him and wrapped her wet arms around him and kissed him hard on the lips, breathing deeply as if she had just sprinted in a race.

If she were not at the beach, she was at the pool. And this gave Nick some time to himself to read the paper and whatever book he happened to pick up that day. He was always reading two or three books at a time, and the girl found it fascinating how he was able to keep the stories and all the characters straight. Each time he picked up the book, it was as if he had never set it down. The girl made him tell her each of the stories up to the point he had read, and the look on her face resembled that of a child when he went into depth about each of the characters and their individual qualities. She especially liked the seemingly unimportant characters who had nothing to do with the plot itself, and Nick often fashioned his own details about them, to her great amusement.

Nick read voraciously. He had decided earlier that year to spend his summer reading. There were stacks of books strewn about the hotel room. Some he had bought, some he had taken from friends when he was at their homes and asked to borrow them. It was going to be difficult knowing which book to return to whom, he thought, so he started writing little notes in each of them on the hotel stationery. The maid had seen the piles of books and had even recommended one in French that she liked to Nick and then brought it by the next day for him. He read it in a few days and gave it back to her with a small rip in one of the pages, and he apologized profusely to her and asked if he could buy her a new copy. She smiled and said that it was not necessary as she had taken it from the hotel library, and no one would notice the small tear.

Nick looked at his watch and saw that it was almost seven o'clock. They were going to meet friends in Monaco for dinner and then they would go to a party there at one of the hotels near the Casino in Monte-Carlo. The *Hermitage*, he believed it was, but he never could be sure, as there was always some party at one of the big hotels. He went to his desk and moved the letters from a pile of papers and mail to the edge where he would see them in the morning and remember to finish addressing them before leaving them with the front desk. With his drink in one hand and his cigarette case in the other, he left the room and caught the elevator to the ground floor to see if he could find the girl.

The party that evening was in one of the suites at the *Hôtel Hermitage* just off from the Casino in Monte-Carlo. Before that, dinner had taken place at nine o'clock at the home of a friend high on the hills above the eastern beaches of Monaco where, the summer before, Nick had watched seaplanes put out the fires on the hills that had engulfed two or three homes. He remembered standing there watching the fires and the planes dropping their water, but even more than that he remembered watching the spectators as they stood eating their ice cream and taking pictures while the fires burned.

On the short cab ride into the city, the girl had turned to him excitedly. "I want to go to the aquarium in Nice!" she'd said. "I saw a poster as I passed the bus stop yesterday. Take me, pleeeease!" She'd dragged this last word out the same way a child would, as if asking for something she knew she would never have.

"Sure," said Nick calmly. He had been busy watching the homes and buildings pass by as they made their way through the streets. It was just starting to get dark, and he adjusted his collar to try and cool off from the warm day.

"Oh, thank you!" she'd replied with a quick, wet kiss to his cheek.

He smiled to himself.

The dinner that evening was no different than any other dinner he had had with friends that summer. Same faces, same conversations. And the party later that night was no different than any other party he had attended. It was the same music, the same drinks, the same pretensions. The only change was that he was preoccupied watching the girl this time. She was quiet and spoke cordially with the other guests, but only when someone spoke to her. Though she had introduced herself again as Eva, she rarely responded to it when someone called her name. Nick felt as if she were out of place, and he wanted to step in and reassure her or take her away. It seemed that she did not know this society or the way these people judged everything about you. But in each instance he sat back and saw that she was fine on her own, especially after a glass or two of champagne that made him more relaxed.

Over the next few days, he started to see the type of girl she was and saw glimpses into her little peculiarities. She wrote things like "Everything is nothing and nothing is everything" on cocktail napkins that he found stuffed in his pockets or on his desk pad in the hotel room. She informed him that she had been engaged twice before but never married and that each time she had said yes to the proposal and knew she didn't mean it—once to a professor of hers, and once to a painter who she had to support until various addictions ruined his originality. Both propositions occurred, apparently, while she was attending a university in the Netherlands. But soon after she revealed this, Nick said the one phrase to her he knew in Dutch, to which she replied only, "Pardon?"

Once, when she was buying a magazine, she insisted that the man behind the counter had given her the incorrect change in her favor; and when he assured her he hadn't, she threw the money on the counter and ran out in tears, leaving the magazine behind. At parties, on more than one occasion, she claimed that she had once sung for the Queen of Denmark but refused to repeat the performance for the other guests, saying only that her throat was a bit scratchy from smoking too many cigarettes before going to sleep last night. One afternoon, when they had passed a church on the train to Nice, she declared, "I am going to start going to church again," and she left it at that without another word. She lacked the ability to wink and instead blinked both eyes at the same time and laughed at herself hysterically for doing so as she repeated the task in the mirror. When Nick asked her to whistle, she did so only after declaring that she had learned how when she was three and that her sister had taught her by having her blow through a soda straw. And when asked to snap her fingers, she performed the task while informing him that she never learned to blow bubbles with her gum and still could not ride a bike.

By her looks, she was no more than twenty, but Nick had always been bad at guessing ages. He himself would be thirty-one in September, and he sensed that she was a bit older than she looked. Due to the constant swimming, her body was fit and thin, and when he lay next to her he could feel her heart beat strongly as she slept. Her arms were slim and long, yet she was small, nearly a foot and a half shorter than Nick himself. Her hair was chopped short above her shoulders and had a feathered look, almost uneven, as if she had cut it herself. She later confirmed this fact for him when she asked for his scissors. Her skin was dark from the sun, but her legs showed thin little scars that seemed to have no cause at all, and she had a small half-moon scar in the center of her forehead that was only noticeable if she turned a certain way in the light. She said she was always bumping into things and that scars showed that a person had truly lived instead of just sitting still and wondering.

These were his observations of her, and it quickly became a pleasant diversion for Nick just to watch her and absorb her qualities. This is what occupied his mind this evening as he caught glimpses of her from across the smoke-filled room after he got swept into a conversation with a man whose wife was a pianist and he and the girl got separated among the crowd. The pianist wore her dark hair curled tight around the sides of her head—a style that for some reason did not please him. Nick distractedly caught the man telling him that he played the piano, too, but that he never learned to read sheet music.

"You play by ear then?" said Nick, coming back to the conversation.

"What's that?"

"You play by ear then?"

There was a pause, as if the man were looking at him for the first time. "I'm not sure. Maybe it's that. I don't know."

"He plays almost as well as I do," the wife chimed in. But Nick could tell she really didn't think so.

Nick was only half-interested in the conversation and took another sip of his drink before losing sight of the girl among the crowd.

In another moment, after a few bumps and pushes among the other guests to make way for the servers and those moving about, Nick found himself speaking with a group of men who were intent on discussing the fate of a politician who had been torn apart in the papers and were decidedly against enjoying themselves there. He countered this by taking a few quick, heavy gulps from the glass of whisky in his hand and asked the waiter to bring more. A minute later, when the drink hit him right, he found that he was able to stomach the conversation that much better.

At that precise moment, above the roar of the crowd, the sound of a glass smashing on the ground pierced the room, and everyone quieted and turned toward the direction of the disturbance. Only the music from the record player in the corner of the room continued. Nick, too, turned his head, and saw the young girl standing a few feet away with a red face. There was no movement or sound from her, and then, in a flash, she burst into tears and ran out of the room.

Before anyone knew what had happened, the voices resumed and the sounds of the party rose to the level they had been a few moments before. Nick quickly excused himself from the present conversation, turned up his glass to get the last of his drink, set it on a table, and headed out the doors in the direction the girl had disappeared.

The doors he went through took him out to a vast open balcony where the warm air that remained from the day hit him forcefully against the cooler air from the hotel suite. Immediately, he saw her there before him, alone, leaning over the balcony, her hair in tangles and her face held firmly in her hands.

"Eva!" he shouted. It was the only time he remembered calling her by her name.

She did not look at him. He only heard a soft whimper come from her small frame. He reached out and touched her delicately on the shoulder.

"Oh…!" She turned and buried her face hard into his chest, almost knocking him back.

She sobbed and mumbled, and after a minute or two he was finally able to understand her.

"...and I didn't mean to throw the glass!" she exclaimed. "He said something mean to me...he said my jewelry looked fake..."

Nick did not say a word.

"...and that my hair made me look like a tramp..."

He remained silent and let her sob. After another minute, she calmed down and let out a long sigh as if her whole body were exhausted. Finally, he spoke softly.

"I'm sure he didn't mean it," he said. "He was probably just drunk. Everyone in there is drunk right now. We're all drunk." But her tears and the fresh air made it so that he soon was not.

"It sounded like he meant it," she replied.

"I'm sure he didn't. People at these parties can be mean. They say things that have no substance."

There was a pause from her. "Well..." she looked at him, "...my jewelry is fake. But he didn't have to say it!"

Nick smiled to himself and quickly straightened his face. She continued.

"A lot of jewelry is fake in there. Half the diamonds in there are just glass!" she went on.

Nick had never thought of that. It was probably true, but he had never even thought of that.

He remembered the napkin he had in his pocket from the drink and handed it to her now that she had stopped crying. The dark makeup around her eyes ran heavily down her cheeks. The girl sniffed a few times and eventually stopped her body from sobbing and shaking. She smiled and reached up to kiss Nick on the side of his lips with a wet face.

"Don't worry about them," he said as he held her slight body tight to his. "They're all frauds themselves. All of them!"

After a few minutes, the girl reached into her purse for a cigarette, and a waiter came up to them to light a match. The three of them were the only ones on the wide balcony.

"Would you like some wine?" the waiter asked. He had two glasses left on his tray.

"Thank you." Nick took both the glasses and handed her one. "Can you leave the bottle?"

"This one is empty. I'll bring another one."

Nick thanked him, and they were again alone. There was quiet now, and the two stared absently out to the water and to the lines of yachts far below. The moon was behind a cloud, but the reflection on the water reached them in a thousand flashes.

The girl moved in front of him and looked up at him seriously. It took a few seconds for Nick to take his eyes away from the distance. He looked down at her and saw her there. It was the first serious look he had ever seen from her.

"Nick?" she said solemnly.

He nodded at her with a sense of confused anticipation.

"Does my hair make me look like a tramp?"

His first reaction was to immediately dismiss this idea, but he held himself for a moment and looked at her curiously. This was not a simple question. She was truly looking to him for an answer. It was as if he held her fragility in his hand, and just one word from him could shatter her entire being.

He smiled, first inwardly, and then to her. When she saw this, she sighed, and he felt her body ease.

"Of course not," he said; and at that moment the waiter returned and began to open the new bottle. Nick stopped him and asked him to leave it there with them, just wanting to be alone with her.

"Merci," he nodded to the waiter as he left them there.

By this time, a few more couples had found their way out onto the balcony. It was a night that was beginning to cool, and the open doors from the party soon brought the music outside.

"I want to get out of here," she finally said to him. They hadn't spoken for several minutes.

"All right. What do you have in mind?"

"I'm hungry. Let's go eat something."

On their way out of the party, Nick put the bottle inside his jacket, and they made their way out of the hotel and through the streets and down the steep hill from the Casino to the harbor below where the yachts and fishing boats sat quietly. They found a small restaurant that still had its lights on, and they went inside to see if they could find some food.

"C'est fermé," the woman inside informed them. "We're closed. We're done serving." The woman looked at Nick

and saw his red eyes and that he was blinking them as if he had opened them for the first time from the darkness.

Nick looked at his watch and saw that it was well past midnight. He looked at the young girl next to him apologetically.

"Do you have anything at all to eat?" he asked the woman in French.

The woman sighed heavily and reached into a wooden box behind the counter. She pulled out a long, thin paper bag that was left over from serving dinner. As he took the bag from her, he felt the still-warm baguette inside.

"Combien?" asked Nick. "How much?"

The woman waved her hand at him. *"Gratuit."*

Nick nodded to her and thanked her. As the two headed out the door, he remembered the bottle of wine in his hand.

"Stay here," he said to the girl. "I'll be right back."

He went back into the restaurant and asked the woman, who was now mopping the floor, if she had a bottle opener. The woman dropped her mop down in the bucket and put her hands on her hips with a look that told Nick that he was now pushing his luck. He saw this and smiled to her with almost a half-wink, and she took the bottle behind the counter. And with the low pop of the cork he knew she was triumphant. He asked for the cork and placed it in his jacket pocket as he gave her a wave and thanked her again on his way out.

"Bonne nuit!" she called to him. "Good night!"

A few steps from the restaurant, he found the girl sitting on the edge of the harbor wall with her shoes off and her feet hanging over the edge toward the water. He joined her there and offered her the bottle of wine. She was finishing chewing a piece of the baguette and mouthed the words "thank you" without saying them and without stopping chewing. She took a big, long drink from the bottle and offered the bread and the bottle to him.

There wasn't much speaking between them. Just a few vacant comments about the water and about this person and that from the party. It was the silence and not their voices that bound them together.

After half an hour they found themselves lying on the thick top of the low concrete wall. The bag that the bread had come in was crumpled up, and the breeze had moved it halfway across the street without them knowing. The empty bottle of wine had found its way into a wide crack further down in the wall and stood upside-down on its neck for the sanitation workers to find the next morning before Monaco and the rest of the coast had awakened.

It was a Saturday, and like all Saturdays that summer Nick found himself next to the hotel pool after lunch with a gin and tonic in his hand, yesterday's unread newspaper draped over the table next to him, and small beads of sweat mixed with chlorine creeping down his skin. The girl was swimming laps, mostly underwater, and he sat there amazed at how long she could hold her breath with such exertion. For the next hour, as the server replaced his empty glasses with fresh ones, he watched her swim and dive, taking the occasional break to sit on the side of the pool and catch her breath. He knew she was watching him, hoping that he was looking at her, but he purposefully turned and looked out across the pool with his dark sunglasses on as though he wanted her to think he was distracted; and in a few moments, he was.

The sun was just starting to go down over the high hills behind him, and he knew the end of the day would soon be here. He thought of the party that was planned for later that night at the *Negresco* in Nice and how he had declined the invitation, due primarily from exhaustion and the need for a break and a good, solid night's sleep. He would not be hurting anyone's feelings; and if he were, the minor offense would quickly be forgotten with the bottle of champagne sent with a handwritten note.

The girl called to him, but he remained there staring off toward the sky. His face was warm from the sun against the coming cool of the evening and the wind that blew from the sea. She came to him and they spoke for a moment, and he decided to go up to the room and lie down on the sofa for a bit. She gave him a wet hug and kissed him on the lips and held him there for a second longer before Nick stepped back and admired the new orange bathing suit he had finally bought for her.

He took his drink with him and took a good look at her as she dove back into the water and stayed under until she had reached the other side of the pool.

He finished drying off in the room and lay down with the last sip of his drink before falling into a half-sleep as he thought about catching the train to Nice tomorrow for lunch before taking her to the aquarium.

Before long, he was hard asleep; and when he finally woke up several hours later, he didn't believe his watch when it read 11:35. He had missed dinner and was hungry, but he didn't have the energy to call down to the kitchen to get something. He washed his face quickly and brushed his teeth in the bathroom and crawled into bed without a shower.

The girl was asleep already with one of the books he had been reading lying open, face-down next to her with the light still on. He slid quietly under the covers and felt her warm, smooth skin against his body. After a few moments with the light off so that his eyes could adjust, he reached over her and kissed her on the cheek and then on the lips and lay there listening to her breathe before falling asleep himself. And in the morning, with the sun peering in between the curtains from the east, he turned toward her in his sleep without noticing that she was gone. And the yellow dress that she had loved so much sat tied up neatly in its cream-colored box on the bed where her body had been, and all that remained of her was the faint smell of perfume and makeup on the pillow.